WHERE GOLD LIES

Jacqueline George

WHERE GOLD LIES
4th edition Copyright © 2025 by J.E. George
ISBN: 978-1-7642150-3-9

Cover design by Jacqueline George
All cover art and logo copyright © 2009 by J.E. George

PUBLISHER
Q~Press Publishing

Table of Contents

Foreword

When I was still a young girl, I chose to spend the summer of my second year in University at my Grandmother's house. I remember it as an Arcadian time. The sun shone every day, I had not a care in the world, my Grandmother's house ran itself as smoothly as the servants could manage, and they treated me as no more than a guest. Nearly three months devoted just to enjoying myself.

At University, I had spent a lot of my time debating with friends the important issues of the day—Socialism, votes for women, the opportunities open to the new King—all of which I treated dreadfully seriously. In fact they took up so much of my time that, at the end of my second year, my tutor had to warn me that I needed some hard serious work on my historical studies if I wanted to graduate the following year. I agreed to undertake some item of historical research during my holidays to demonstrate my ability and seriousness. Still with no idea on just what to study, I reached my Grandmother's at the end of June, looking forward to three months of country living.

Grandmother was an old woman by then (already in her nineties and she died shortly afterwards), but still as sharp as ever. She saw what I needed and artfully put in front of me something that was bound to seize my imagination. She did not go about it directly but merely asked me to try and catalogue a chest of papers from the attic.

The chest contained bundles of letters, mostly dealing with the renting of her estate properties, and the various legal matters that come up in the countryside. Those were dry, dusty and completely uninteresting. I also found a bundle of love letters from an Army officer stationed in India, a love affair that had ended when the officer died of fever. I liked those, but I found it difficult to imagine my grandmother as the glowing young girl in those worn papers.

The document I eventually came to, the one Grandmother knew I would not be able to put down again, is the one that follows here.

I remember quite clearly the first time I held it. I pulled it from its waxed cloth cover and took it to the brighter light of the attic window. It had no cover, just good quality paper punched on its left-hand edge and bound together with a very faded blue ribbon. The first page looked very worn, scraped and dirtied by handling. It had been written in a firm and open script, in faint brown ink. I could hardly read the front page, and it was not until I had turned the leaf that I began to realise what I had found.

The papers contained an account of his early life at sea, written by my great-great-grandfather Richard Brown. I later looked for his records and found that he had ended his days as the priest of Hinton St Anne in the year 1821. He must have written the account around the end of the century (the eighteenth century) and he addressed it to his daughter, Grandmother's mother. It all seemed terribly long ago, but the fact that the people in the story were my ancestors was enough to keep my attention for a little while. What held it right to the end, however, was the story the old pages told.

The young Richard Brown, before he became a priest, had been a pirate and sailed upon the Spanish Main. What an idea to conjure with! What a delight to have such an infamous man in my family tree. In the end, Destiny had led him away from the calling of pirate and he had left the sea to become a parish priest. He had one daughter, Great-grandmother Rose, and had told her nothing of his past.

Then a chance event had brought him to the point of confessing everything to his daughter. A naval captain who had known him in his days as a pirate arrived at his house. The Captain did not recognise him, and all would have been well if he had not fallen in love with Rose. He and Rose wanted to marry and poor Richard Brown faced the impossibility of concealing his early life from his daughter any longer. That was why he had sat down and written the whole tale on the pages I held.

Imagine my delight when I found that he had not been just an ordinary pirate. I had read of him before, as have most people in England, in the book *Treasure Island*. Richard Brown had been there at the time. He was one of the wicked men who came so badly out of that story.

I threw myself into researching the background of Richard Brown's account, and by the end of the summer had produced a paper supporting the truth of it. My paper was sound but perhaps a little more exciting than Oxford tutors are accustomed to. I did not mind. It kept me academically respectable and (much more fun) gave me a reputation to dine out on. I had resolved to have it published but by the time I had got halfway through that tiresome process, many events conspired to delay it. I had graduated more or less comfortably, taken a tour around Europe and got married. I started a family and then the Great War intervened. Thank God, my husband eventually returned to me from France, and we got busy putting our lives back on an even keel.

Babies are not great friends to literature and until the children had grown up a little I rarely thought of Richard Brown. Now, however, my excuses are exhausted and I have at last managed to see the story published in book form. I hope you will come to like Richard Brown, and even Long John Silver, as much as I do.

Joan Downey, Paignton, 1931

Death in Savannah

I write this account of events long past because a story I thought had ended has come to life again. It threatens to entangle you in deeds and memories you are too young to remember. I do not even know if I want you to read this account; I am at a standstill. Providence has provided that Captain Hawkins should come to my house and ask for your hand. I would be happy to see you accept him, but if you do, I must tell you things about your upbringing that I have kept hidden for many years. I fear they may hurt you deeply.

Perhaps as a modern girl you will find this tale as exciting as a novel or a play. As your father I could not approve of that. Both your grandfather and I were thoroughly wicked and odious at that time. Since then, I have tried hard to amend my life and in some fashion pay for my sins. I would wish that your grandfather did the same wherever he travelled to, but knowing him as I did, I doubt it. I will let you read on, and may God and your own good conscience be your guide.

This account in some ways reflects the curious book that Doctor Livesey published in the name of Hawkins, and in some ways differs from it. Livesey sought to hide Treasure Island not only by withholding its latitude and longitude, but also by transforming its tropical flora into something much nearer home. So the coconut palms became pines, and holm oaks replaced the much more useful breadfruit trees. He added snakes, and dispersed the clouds of mosquitoes and other biting insects. An effective disguise, for you would be hard put to identify the place if you sailed right by it. Not even the hills have remained in their assigned stations.

Other differences are tricks of memory, and here I am at my weakest for I write many years after the Doctor. I am an old man now and have an old, worn brain. My memory plays tricks on me, and I begin to wonder what was true and what imagined. Believe me, the time of which I write is as clear in my mind as a summer's day. I have only to close my eyes and I can hear the sounds, smell the smells and feel the deck heave under my feet. Some things are gone, however, names especially. But all the names I recall I will put down clearly. Most of them will be dead by now, and you are not likely to publish the others abroad.

I dare say Hawkins would disagree with much of what I will write. For your own sake and your future peace, I beg you will not show this to him. There is nothing to be gained by upsetting him, and I do not believe he could keep it secret. Can you imagine such an expansive nature labouring not to let the cat out of the bag? It is better that he never knows. He has Livesey's account in mind anyway, and I doubt that mine would find favour.

Just as two men may meet on a certain day in the market square and next year admit the meeting but disagree on the day, the weather, the colour of the other's coat, so Livesey and I disagree about details. But for the most part his account accords closely with mine, always understanding that they were written from different sides of the mast. Enough of this. I will philosophise no longer but set down the truth of the tale and let you judge.

The tale starts, I suppose, on the day Flint died in Savannah of the effects of yellow fever and too much rum. I was a member of his crew, a young man of some twenty years answering to the name of Dick. A full twelve of those years had been spent at sea with Flint, starting as a cabin boy and becoming in time a seaman able to reef and steer. How I came to join Flint and the events that filled those years is another tale, and I will pass them by. It is enough that I describe myself as young, full of vigour, and a pirate. In my time with Flint I had sailed many sea miles, ranged over three oceans, and visited more ports than you can imagine. My trade of piracy meant that I had committed many wicked deeds, and seen many more. I was very sinful and very ignorant.

Flint died on board his ship Walrus moored at the quayside in Savannah. He had raved the evening through, cursing and shouting for rum. By morning his unquiet soul had passed on, undoubtedly to the eternal fires. A terrible thunderstorm had accompanied his departure from this world, a fitting eulogy to a wicked and bloody man. The morning came soft, clear and sunny, washed clean by the violence of the night.

The Walrus was a fine ship, light and well rigged. She could outrun any merchant ship and most men o' war. Whatever faults Flint had (and he had many), he did not stint on caring for his ship. Our stores were kept full of paint and cordage, and our stock of sails would have cost a fortune had we purchased them. Of course the stores, as with the victuals, we mostly looted from our victims. We had a fine crew too, all as bound to the Walrus as a tenant to his farm. There was no fear of us skipping off when we came to port. Firstly, of course, no other ship would have taken us once they heard where we had come from. And secondly, the Walrus suited us. We had grown accustomed to her ways and liked the life, which is a terrible thing to say.

So there we were, on the morning after Flint's death, tied up to an old and rather shaky wharf some distance from the main quay of Savannah.

The sun had begun to make the morning hot and heavy, and we did not yet have the benefit of a breeze to stir the water and bring some freshness. The crew was loafing about on deck waiting for something to happen, and discussing to where we might sail. We gossiped that we would soon make sail to leave this ill-omened place, and bury Flint at sea where he belonged. We were waiting for the ship's officers Billy Bones (mate) and Long John Silver (quartermaster) to tell us what to do.

As it turned out, we were too late. People say that bad news travels fast, and the news of Flint's death had been heard in certain influential breakfast rooms around the town. As we stood day-dreaming, a file of soldiers marched onto the quay led by a smart young officer. The town authorities and merchant who had been Flint's protectors and chandlers had moved to protect their investment.

Leaving a sentry at the foot of the gangplank, the officer led his men aboard. He dropped heavily off the ship's rail and stood looking us over. He was tall and fair, no older than I but with the bearing of a General. In his smart red coat and fine neck cloth, he looked a complete contrast to his surroundings. He looked about him disdainfully and did not approve of what he saw.

"Flint is dead," he stated. "Where is your first officer?"

We looked at one another like sheep until Long John, stepping out of the cabin, answered him. "I reckon that's me you'd be wanting, Sir. John Silver, quartermaster, at your service."

"Mr. Silver," said the officer, looking at him more closely. "I've heard of you." He looked pointedly at the soldiers now lining the rail. "Well, Mr. Silver, I have orders from the harbourmaster to impound this vessel. I also have orders to imprison any crewman still in Savannah at mid-day. Kindly lead your men ashore."

The silence that followed this command seemed long. It was broken by the sergeant cocking his musket. His men followed suit.

Long John could only acquiesce. "Step ashore, lads," he growled. "This pup's masters have no more use for you now." The sergeant tensed but was held by a gesture from his officer. "Move!" ordered Long John and we filed ashore.

Once ashore past the sentry, we turned to watch Long John being handed down the gangplank by two of our crew. The Walrus had been our home for several years and you may imagine a wave of great sadness sweeping over us as we comprehended that both she and our Captain had been taken from us.

"D---- take those lobsters," muttered Israel Hands. "I've twenty dollars still aboard."

"What, Israel?" cried someone. "You've money of your own and you were letting us keep you in grog the other night?"

I sympathised with him. I had several silver dollars and an emerald of great size hidden behind a knee in the hold. The stone was my pride and joy, though I don't recall what I thought to do with it. Sell it, probably, and buy a ship of my own. How young men can dream.

"There'll be a few purses aboard, I'll be bound," put in Chips Morgan, one of the old hands. "But what about Flint's cabin? There's a sight more hidden away there. That officer will be poking his nose into every corner just now."

"And much good may it do him!" laughed Long John. "For he'll find nothing. Billy Bones was there before him."

Long John laughed again. "He's done us proper. While you drunken turtles were swinging in your hammocks, King Billy the Fourth shoved off in the jolly boat. I saw him come out of the cabin and he left the place in a wild tangle too. He wasn't after no dollars, though. I doubt he'd have found any, even if he was. He was after Flint's chart of the Island, that's what he wanted. He's taken his chest, and if he doesn't have the chart along with him, then you may use me for a sinker."

The Island. That was the place the world now knows as Treasure Island, where Flint had buried his evil wealth. The story had gone like this. About a year or two before he died, Flint and the Walrus had struck upon the chance of a lifetime. We had been cruising off the ports of the South Americas looking for likely victims, and having a very thin time of it. In two months we had done no more than steal enough food to keep us alive. Now we were heading back to the West Indies to see if our luck would change. Then one dawn the helmsman passed the word and we tumbled out of our hammocks to the hushed voice of Long John telling us to stay below and keep quiet.

He stood on deck and called forward to us all that was happening. It seemed that out of the dawn was sailing the largest Spanish galleon we could imagine. Beating towards the Walrus on a parallel course, she would pass only a short distance upwind of us. All aboard her appeared to be sleeping. We waited in the dark of the fo'c'sle, not too worried. The Walrus would no doubt pass as harmless, and that was the best we could hope for. In no case could we try to attack such a grand vessel, and she would be unlikely to waste any precious time with us.

"She'll be a-beam of us shortly," Long John called down. "What lubbers they are! We could be a fleet of the King's ships and they'd be no wiser."

We heard Flint moving about and a whispered conversation with Long John and Billy Bones. Then Billy came rushing in calling for Israel Hands, our gun captain.

"Get the starboard guns clear away, then wait." was the message he brought. "Don't let no one see you about it, neither. We're going to have a go at them. But don't run 'em out 'til Flint calls. Shot or grape, it don't signify." He rushed off again and let us to our work. The guns were on deck, in full view of our adversary. Israel set four of us to crawl out of the fo'c'sle under the shelter of the railing and ready the guns.

Soon Billy hurried back. "Grape into the aft cabin and shot at the rudder. And don't miss or you'll wish for the D---- to carry you off."

And again. "Soon as I call, you larboard hands to the mainsheets. Standby. We'll be going about then run the guns out and shoot. You won't get no second chance, Israel Hands, so make it count."

"Just you worry about sailing this barky," Israel returned, "An' I shall worry about the guns." We always kept two of the guns on each side loaded with grape-shot and the other three with round-shot. Not that we used them much. A shot across the bows of our prey was generally enough to achieve our purpose.

Israel paused in his organising of the gun crews to call, "How far off will she be?"

This time Long John answered. "One or two cables. And the cabin lights is all of two and a half fathoms off the water."

More than two fathoms. This ship they were looking at was clearly no cockleshell. It was all very well to fire into such a ship, but how could we go about boarding her?

Billy Bones clattered in again. "There's cutlasses in the starboard scuppers, and pistols, but you'll have to load them. D--- you! What's all this dunnage? Get it forward." The men clearing the guns had thrown sweeps, hen coops, buckets aside, and now the port battery looked like a wood-yard. Keeping as much out of sight as we could we started to clear them as well. They might be needed.

The crew stood waiting in the dark in a state of twisted nervousness. The men about me were nagging incessantly at their belts, their knives, anything. One man took of his shoes, the better to climb in bare feet, and then changed his mind and put them back on again. We felt desperate to start.

12

The deck started to heave beneath us as we went about, and Billy shouted "Larboard watch, larboard watch." We tumbled out and ran to our stations. My place was in the maintop. The galleon seemed truly enormous and I looked up at masts towering above me. Flint had taken the helm and was busy cutting towards her stern. One by one, the guns rumbled out, and the wall that was the Spanish ship came nearer and nearer.

As we started to round her quarter Israel fired. He did not disappoint us and we saw the great rudder shatter. Then we were passing the cabin lights. Two white faces, no doubt just shaken from their cots, appeared at the windows and disappeared as the glass dissolved under two charges of grape.

"D--- me, there's no stern chasers!" I heard Long John shout nearby. "They can't touch us!"

Flint was screaming, wild with blood and destruction "More grape, more grape. Israel! More grape in the cabin from the larboard guns." We continued to swing round moving our head across the wind, and as the rudderless galleon also brought her head slowly up into the wind, I saw he would indeed have another opportunity to fire into the cabin.

Billy sent men over to the port guns, and I too climbed down onto the smoky deck. Our deck was a vision of the Inferno. The wind had quickly cleared the smoke but not the disorder as we secured one battery in order to use the other. From every hand came the squealing of gun carriages and the shouts of straining men as guns ran in and out. Then Israel was shouting as he ran from gun to gun, laying them roughly. No time to aim now. He held an instant of tense quiet as he waited for his gun to bear, then he stood back and stabbed his linstock at the touch hole. With flash and thunder the gun bucked back against its britching, the other four following.

"Har!" he roared. "That'll have them. Run 'em in." He called up to Billy, "Grape or shot, what'll you have?"

"Grape, grape. Into her ports." Flint had loosed his sheets and was using the way we still had from our short run down wind to lay us along the galleon's starboard side. As we began to close, a gun port in that castle wall started to open. It dropped, and then lifted firmly up, showing its red-painted maw with the gun still inboard. One of Israel's guns barked its charge into the shadow and the port dropped shut again in a whirl of splinters. A voice from behind the port raised a high animal screaming.

As the Walrus rubbed gently into place we were off, roaring in our madness. We flew up to find the Spanish deck empty. The deck hands had fled. "The cabins," ordered Billy. "Get as many prisoners as you can out here. Don't miss no one." And he started to shout in Spanish down to the gun deck.

We swept into the cabins. In truth I recall very little of what was there. The grape had torn the partitions to pieces. In the great cabin a woman knelt beside a bloody groaning man. Despite the devastation around she seemed unhurt. There were female screams coming from one of the smaller cabins as George Merry and Chips Morgan drove two more women out on deck. I opened one cabin and found two dead men among the wreckage.

"Out. Out on deck!" Billy was shouting. "Bring 'em out here." So back out we went, with our prisoners. We brought the Captain, the man from the great cabin, suffering from a fearsome splinter in his thigh. Three women, all unharmed, and two officers, one of them nursing a broken arm.

We had not been aboard long for as we returned Israel's gun crews were just mounting the rail. Billy grabbed the uninjured officer and shook him roughly, shouting at him all the while in Spanish. I could just make out (having picked up a little of that language) that he was threatening murder if the man did not co-operate. Wisely, the officer started to shout below in a tremulous voice, calling on the men to surrender. A strong voice from below asked for the Captain, and the officer replied that the Captain still lived. There was silence from below.

"The swabs are running out a gun," Long John's voice called from the deck of the Walrus. "Stop them, or they'll have the mast."

When I ran to the rail to see what was afoot, I could see we were in trouble. One of the great guns had already been run out. The galleon being so much higher than the Walrus, it pointed out across the deck. Long John, his crutch hanging from its lanyard about his neck, was standing on the railing and reaching up to jam his cutlass deep into the gun. Like a cat, he dropped to the deck and with rare speed hopped clear, trying to untangle his crutch as he went. He had got well away when a thunderous crash told that the gun had burst. The deck above it tore open, timber and splinters whirring up into the rigging.

All on deck flinched instinctively as the fragments pattered down around us. As we straightened up our ears were filled with the awful roaring of some poor injured sailor below.

Flint appeared unshaken. "Israel, take four men and get below. Hold your pistols on them until I call you." Looking around, he picked on the officer with the broken arm. "Billy, make him tell us what's on board."

Billy, never a man to shrink from such a task, shook the man violently by the shoulder before demanding gold from him. The man groaned deeply and looked set to faint, but the effect of Billy's shaking was felt most by the women who screamed in unison and then reverted to weeping hysterically. The oldest of the three then started to shout at the Captain (she was undoubtedly his wife) and I caught the words *oro* and *tesoro*. Both of them meant a great deal to us—gold and treasure.

If the Captain had not been defeated by grapeshot and cutlass, he had certainly been out-manoeuvred by his wife. Resignedly he admitted to twenty-seven chests of the Spanish king's treasure, and more belonging to the passengers.

Strangely, it did not seem in the least unusual that our small band should hold the crew of such a large ship at pistol point. We accepted it, and so did they. Flint had the seamen brought on deck and seated where they could be commanded by two swivel guns mounted on the railings of the poop deck. A party of Indians were set to hauling the chests out of their cabin aft. It took only moments to pass these heavy little chests down to the Walrus. Then we cut the galleon's halyards to give ourselves time to get clear, and we were off.

The crew wanted to open the chests there and then, but Flint would have none of that. "Victuals first, my lads, and then we'll see."

Now the custom on the Walrus was to divide our spoils just as soon as we could. A system of shares had grown up—one third for the ship, one third for her captain, and one third for the crew. So once we had finished our salt pork and beans, everyone came on deck to witness the division into three. First we opened all the chests and many contained money in leather bags, all neatly labelled. These we readily split into three heaps. The other chests yielded ornaments and jewellery, strings of pearls and church plate. A beautiful sight they made, scattered on the rough deck, glittering in the sunlight.

By the time we had finished we had made three heaps, each about as wide across as a carriage wheel. Their foundations were of money-bags and we topped them off with the other items, lying on the cloth wrappings in which they had been stored.

"Ain't that a pretty sight?" chuckled Flint in a fine good humour. "Now which will you be taking?" Custom also held that the crew should have the privilege of choosing which third they would take. We crowded around Israel all giving our opinion on which would be preferable. Reaching agreement was easy. We all wanted to hold treasure in our own hands, and we did not care too much which pile it should be.

We made our choice, and the heaps for Flint and the ship were packed back in their chests. Then the whole business started again as we divided up our third. Long John and Billy got four shares a-piece. Israel got three, and the cook and the carpenter two each. The rest of us received one share. Any boys or slaves (we had none just then) would have got a half share each. So again the booty was divided into equal shares, and the most junior crew member allowed to choose first.

I chose a lot that consisted of two bags of silver, a purse of gold pieces and a large shining emerald the like of which I have never seen. I believe now it would have been worth much more than the Walrus, if only the right king or prince could be found to take it. I am afraid my bags of money did not last me long. Young men have a great tendency to waste without thought and my gold and silver soon went, leaving me with nothing to show for it. The emerald I kept, as much for its beauty as for its value.

But now I was separated from my emerald by the distance from the Savannah quayside to the Walrus. It had gone forever, along with all my shipmates' savings. We vented our frustration on Billy Bones, cursing and wondering where he had gone. Then someone suggested setting out to look for him.

"Belay that!" ordered Long John. "The Factor sailed for Charleston on the tide and you may lay to it that our Billy is tucked up in a fine cabin a-reading of the chart just now."

We had all been taken aback by the events of the last moment and as sheep turn to their shepherd, so we turned to our quartermaster. Even here we had no succour. Long John cut us adrift.

"You'll have to take care of yourselves, melads. I've a friend will hide me here. Just as well, for I'd be left far behind your two legs.

"If I was in your shoes, I'll tell you what I'd do. I'd march out of town making as much noise about it as I could. Make out I was bound for Mexico or Port Royal. Then I'd steal a cockle or anything that could take me up the coast, along with a couple of these here Indian canoes. Lay up the cockle across from the harbour, and use the canoes to run in to the Walrus after the moon sets. If you keep it quiet and don't cut no throats, you'll get your purses and no questions asked. But don't you go sticking no one or trying to cut the Walrus out, or you'll have all the ships them sainted merchants and tobacco factors can raise sent out after you. Just cut and run, lads, cut and run. Do it nicely, and you'll all be square.

"Now, look'ee. Get up to Charleston, and try and get your hands on Billy. Or better still, get hold of the chart. But I doubt you will. Our Billy's too fly by half. The Factor is a trim barky and he'll be in

Charleston in no time. An' he'll ship out just as soon as he can. But Long John knows where he's bound. Long or short, he's for Bristol, or maybe Plymouth. He has a soft spot for the Old Country, has our Billy. That's where we'll get him. One day he'll pull his nose out of his grog pot just in time to see Long John setting up to feed his liver to the gulls, d--- his rotten heart.

"Make it Bristol, lads. Keep close hauled and ask for Long John just as soon as you step ashore. I'll have space for you to stow your duds. And d--- me for a Dutchman if we don't clap onto Billy smartly, and roast him 'til he sings. Make it Bristol, lads."

He spun on his crutch and swung off. As he stepped out, there was a rush of feathers and with a loud squawk, Flint's parrot crashed onto his shoulder. Without looking round, Long John marched on. The parrot swayed on his shoulder, croaking and whispering into his ear. Off he went through the crowd of gawpers that had gathered on the quayside. They opened to let him pass, and closed behind him. We felt it was truly a day for great losses.

Please excuse me. Already I am several pages into my story and you still do not know how it concerns you. The truth is that Long John was your grandfather. I am sorry, but there it is. He was your grandfather, and I have been telling very little about him. Livesey wrote a great deal of him, and painted him very black. Did he paint a fair portrait? I am bound to say that, as far as it went, it was not too unkind. Especially in his prime when he had both his legs, Long John was a rogue, a black-hearted pirate who cared little for God's creatures. His soul was stained with the blood of many a poor man foolish enough to stand in his way. God knows that our crew were mostly mindless fools. They gave as little thought to killing a man as you do to squashing a horse-fly, and Long John was their quartermaster.

Both in body and character he stood head and shoulders above the rest of us, and above Flint too. He was a handsome man and a fine sailor. He had black hair, bound up in a short tarred pigtail. His eye was clear and he had an air of breeding about him. Flint trusted him with any difficult job that came up. I believe Flint would never have a clever man or a strong one as his mate, and that may be why he and Long John kept their distance. But when the need arose, Long John was the man called on. He was also the only man Flint feared.

For us youngsters in the crew, Long John was someone to look up to and emulate. We would jump to any order he gave, and accept blows and rebukes without rancour. I treasured every bit of praise he gave. It never occurred to us to question the order of things, the Captain in his cabin and

Long John slinging his hammock along with the cook and the carpenter. Why did Long John never cross Flint and take over the ship? Why did he stay content to take orders from a man who feared him?

Looking back now, I can see your grandfather had already embarked on a different voyage to the rest of us. At sea he pulled the crew along in his wake when we had Satan's work to do, but then he cut us adrift on shore. Not for him the wild carousing in taverns and bawdy houses that wasted the substance of the rest of us. Once in port Long John kept to himself until the time came to ship again.

I believe it suited him very well to have Flint as captain, and to have Flint's name painted in bloody letters up and down the Caribbean. He made only one voyage as captain, and I believe that was his last before he left the sea and disappeared. For the rest, he stood in the background and we, poor fools, stood in his shadow.

So where did he go when he left us all aground on that steaming day in Savannah? Where did he swing off to through the crowd? The answer to that was his great secret. He stepped back into his other life. He marched back to your grandmother Sally. Long John might be a pirate at sea, but in port he was a simple, respectable sea-farer living with his wife and daughter. It may seem strange to you that a man as prominent and identifiable as Long John could hide himself ashore, especially in a busy port. Things are different across the sea. Savannah is a great mix of black and white, slave and master, Spanish and English. Like most of the ports around the West Indies, it can sell you anything you can imagine. If you could see the silks from China, the lace from France, dainty ladies boots from Spain, I am sure you would never wish to go to Exeter again. Ships are always coming and going, discharging cargoes from England and the countries of Europe and the South Americas, and sailing out east or south fully laden.

The people too, come and go. The life of the port changes with the seasons and the years. The inhabitants no more belong to Savannah than the muddy water that swirls in and out of the harbour twice daily.

Even His Majesty's servants are temporary. The fine lieutenants and commodores, the revenue officers, the governor himself, do not belong in Savannah. As soon as they have lined their sea-chests with the pickings of the wharfs and counting-houses, they set sail for old England where their money is as good as the next man's, indeed often better, being minted from fine Spanish gold. And any poor soul obliged by slavery or indenture to remain will soon be carried off by yellow fever, black jack, ague, flux or any of the other myriad plagues waiting to strike down those whose blood is not accustomed to the climate.

Long John was able to live unmarked, hidden away in Savannah, or Port O' Spain or any of the other ports in which Sally set herself up. All the time he was salting away the money that we ship-mates scattered to any tavern-keeper or pretty girl that would help us spend it. Where did Long John keep his gold? He was too clever to stuff his mattress with it, or hang it about his wife's neck. I learnt later that many a tun of tobacco loaded for Bristol, or rum for Boston, belonged to Long John. In fact, there is today in Bristol a ship-owning family - one of the finest - that would be obliged to stand at the door, cap in hand, to welcome the ghost of your grandfather, should he ever decide to pay a visit.

He was already a man of substance when Livesey met him, but he had a dream and he needed Flint's treasure to bring that dream ashore. Poor Billy Bones! He hated and feared Long John but a twist of his simple mind made him steal Flint's chart, knowing he would let loose a demon from Hell on his trail.

For us gathered at the foot of the gang-plank, the most important thing on our minds was to get back on board. Israel opened the door by shouting to the sergeant that we wanted to come back and collect our duds. The sergeant was a hard nut and declined to answer, but then the officer came out of the cabin. After a moment's consideration he ordered, "Let them aboard, sergeant. Two minutes below, then back on deck."

The sergeant swallowed. "You heard the lieutenant. Get below on the double and back in two minutes."

We scrambled aboard and hurriedly wrapped our valuables into what good clothes we possessed. Then climbed back up to the deck, to face a ring of hard-faced marines with muskets levelled. What green fools we were! At the head of the gang-plank we and our bundles were searched, and we lost everything of value. The spectators on the quay loved the circus, and cheered each new find of gold or gems flourished aloft by the marines. Once stripped, we were bundled off the ship to shrieks of laughter.

With our tails between our legs, we pushed through the crowd and made for the road north.

Bristol Bound

I travelled to Charleston with a young crew member, Caspar. We had been close friends aboard ship, being of an age with each other. Caspar had joined the Walrus by way of the army. He had deserted in Barbados after listening to our tales in a tavern there, and had found the relative freedom much more to his taste. The army had let him grow tall, strong and curly-haired, and leaving early as he did, he brought no dull military subservience with him. Now he had been both a soldier and a sailor, he made a fine companion for the journey, just as knowing by land as he was by sea. We left the others in a wood just outside Savannah and resolved to push on to Bristol as fast as we could go.

It was a long walk to Charleston, as far, I suppose, as from here to London. However, we were young, and soon shook off the distress of losing both home and fortune. With light hearts we marched off, bearing all our worldly goods on our backs, that is to say, the clothes in which we stood. In addition we had our knives (no sea-man is ever without a sharp knife), pipes and tobacco, and precious little else. Caspar had a pair of fine boots, his pride whenever ashore, and he wore them around his neck to protect them from any hurt. I walked in rope slippers that lasted but a few days.

I find it hard after all these years to recall exactly how we managed to stay alive. No doubt the gardens we passed furnished most of our food. I do recall a hard day's work unloading corn from a barge in return for a square meal and a river ride. That was dusty work, and Caspar's black hair turned quite white with the dust of it. I can see him now standing down in the shallow hold of the barge, covered in dust and complaining of the weight of the sacks. Being slighter, I had an easier task. I was in the sunlight working with a Negro slave to swing the bags up onto the rail. Still, times cannot have been too hard, or they would stay clearer in my mind.

We trotted into Charleston on a fine morning and made for the quay. Immediately, we set about finding a ship, for a sailor without a ship is quite as stranded as a fish on the river bank. His ship is his home, and until he can call himself and his mates by the name of a respectable ship, he is a lost soul indeed.

Cautious of carrying the name of the Walrus with us, we agreed on a tale of leaving a ship some months before to view the Americas. And now having run out of money, we were back to the sea. Charleston had several likely looking ships at the quay, and we went quickly from one to the next asking for a place. We were turned back from the gangway of each.

It seemed the city fathers of Charleston looked very narrowly at taverns and the other amusements that sailors usually consider vital to life ashore. As a consequence, it was a bit of a sour place. Few sailors were tempted to jump ship and leave empty berths for us.

Standing amid the bustle of loading and discharging, provisioning and watering, our feeling of dejection must have shown. A boatman called up to us, asking if we were looking for a place. This gentleman did not look altogether straight and perhaps we should have been less ready to accept his offer to run us over to a fine ship just fitting out for Bristol. As things stood, we were without other appointments, and we let him row us round to a nasty, muddy creek where lay the American Providence, fitting out for Bristol just as he had said.

Laying us alongside, he motioned us up to the deck. We stepped aboard amid a tangle of spars, blocks and cordage. Obviously fitting out still had some way to go.

"Good morning! Good morning! Now here's a brace of fine young gentlemen." A short, red-faced individual in a black clerk's coat and linen that badly needed laundering came bustling up to us. "Come to join the Providence? A fine ship, fine ship, none better. Good victuals, dry berths, a happy ship. Couldn't do better, not this side of your mother's hearth. Couldn't do better. What did your mothers call you, lads? What are your names? Come on, make your mark and collect your shilling. Fine lads, couldn't do better!"

This amazing flow of praises alternately of the ship and ourselves, along with much more that I shall not try to set down, was delivered at such a speed that the gentleman did not seem to draw breath. Although he must have done, for he kept up the flow until he had ushered us to the cabin. A glance over the rail showed our boatman rowing rapidly away, presumably by prior arrangement. Caspar and I looked uncertainly at each other and, overwhelmed by our host, we put our names in the ship's register. The flow of blandishments ebbed, and we stepped outside.

"Ah, here is Mr. Doughty, your bo'sun. Mr. Doughty, take these two shillings and make sure you write them down in your slop book for these two young lads. Off you go then, and Mr. Doughty will show you the ropes."

So commenced one of the busiest periods of work I can remember. We rigged, ballasted, and watered the ship prior to kedging her over to the wharf to take on our cargo of tobacco. If the work was hard and long, at least the food was sufficient, and as more hands were signed up, we started to resemble a crew. Doughty was a hard man o'war's man, but fair enough and not over fond of the rope's end.

Loading the tuns of tobacco was the job of a longshore crew, but that did not mean that we sailors could have the liberty of a stroll around town. Indeed, guards stood on the wharf to make sure that none of us would try to stretch his legs ashore and disappear before we sailed. We kept busy working over the spare tackle, and helping the sail maker check and repair the storm-sails. On our final afternoon in port, Caspar and I were on the poop helping the sail maker leech a new storm trysail when an owner's party came aboard, along with the Captain and some passengers.

Generally speaking, there is nothing will prick a captain more than to be in port with the owners aboard. Afloat, the captain is the lord of the manor, holding sway over the ship and the very lives of his crew. Many take on the airs and aspect of a king, and not a few allow Satan to tempt them into acting the part of Deity for their tiny universe. However, when they return to port, even these captains must revert to ordinary mortals. When the owner comes on board, the captain is pressed between acting as a servant (which indeed he is) on the one hand, and on the other maintaining his customary regal dignity towards the crew. It is a job that few captains do well, and most scheme to rush the owners into the cabin as soon as possible. Lavish hospitality is provided to keep them there throughout their stay.

Our owners did not allow themselves to be kidnapped, and induced the Captain to lead them onto the poop deck where we knelt working on our sail.

"Keep working!" he ordered sharply as we jumped to our feet, no doubt hoping to discourage the party from lingering. We quickly bent to our work again and continued uneasily. We felt the weight of the owners' eyes on our backs. There were two children with the party, a young boy and a girl of nine or ten years.

"Oh, look, Mama!" cried the girl. "They are sewing." She ran to the rail and called down to her mother. "Do come up, Mama. The sailors are sewing up here."

We could hear the muted protests of the lady as she was persuaded to come up to the poop and inspect the strange sight of men sewing. "Look how big their needles are, Mama. And the thread. And why do they use those funny things on their hands instead of thimbles?"

After a muffled consultation, the lady decided an interpreter was needed. "Harry, come here!" One of the owners grouped around the

Captain changed in an instant from a Man of Business and hurried over. (It seemed that even Owners have Masters.) "Harry, ask these men what they are doing."

While Caspar struggled to make himself understood, I made myself as small as possible, and stared at the deck in the hope of avoiding notice. At that moment, the sound of a struggle and a quiet imprecation drew my attention. Then above the level of the poop deck appeared an elegant tricorn hat, and below it the cheerful, brown face of Long John Silver, surging rapidly upwards as he fought his way onto the poop.

Fortunately, I was struck dumb by surprise. He, thinking much faster than I, fixed me with a look of such ferocity that I stayed dumb. I elbowed Caspar who had yet to notice our old quartermaster.

Silver marched up to the owner who was questioning us. To my surprised ears came a slightly more educated version of Silver's voice saying "Why, Harry! Here's a thing. I've promised the mothers of these boys to keep an eye out for them and here they are, shipped on the Providence. Stand up, my boys, stand up." We jumped up and stood sheepishly, not knowing what to say or do. "Are you keeping busy, boys? Are you doing your duty?"

The Captain had come up. "Do you know these men, Captain Silver?"

"Indeed I do. And their families. A fine pair of young men, and I promised their mothers I would see them well clothed and well fed if I saw them at all. Are you well, boys? Do you have oilskins?"

Here the Captain forestalled him. "Jones," he called, "have the slops been issued?"

Jones showed his mettle, answering this prompt by assuring the Captain that the slops would be issued that very evening, once the vessel was under sail. "Sailors are well cared for on my ship, Captain Silver," the Captain stated proudly. "A willing sea-man need have no fear."

"I'll wager you'll find them willing," said Silver with emphasis. "I'm convinced they'll do their duty." He marched off leaving us to our work.

That evening we weighed anchor and, sure enough, were issued with a complete set of the best the slop chest had to offer. We did not know if we should accept such finery, for a sailor must pay for all he is given. The wages for a voyage across the Atlantic were quite likely to be less than the cost of our clothes, and we would inevitably be in debt when the time came to leave the ship in Bristol. Doughty re-assured us that the clothes had been charged to the owners' account by "the gentleman with one leg, he being one of them, you see". Long John was a part owner! We took the oilskins and warm clothes with elation.

We saw little of Long John during the voyage. We had generally left the deck by the time the passengers were up and about. From the masthead we might see him on the poop with his wife, a tall Creole lady, and strikingly pretty daughter of fourteen or fifteen years. We had no opportunity to talk. He was an owner and a passenger, and we were but sailors. It is strange to reflect that a ship, a tiny island afloat on a hostile ocean, should divide itself so completely into two parts.

Our voyage across the Atlantic was fast but uneventful. We had sailed at the end of the season, and made our way up the Bristol Channel in a fine autumn gale. You may imagine that Caspar and I were eager to leap ashore and search for Billy Bones. We gave no thought to the daily necessities of food and a roof over our heads. We knew Long John would provide, our confidence in him even being heightened by seeing him in his new station.

You have never travelled on a ship and here am I telling a tale that spends a good deal of time in and out of ships. So let me slow down and try to describe a little of what we saw and did. We were sailing into Bristol because, though you may not know it, Bristol is the most significant port in England. Some may say that honour falls to London, but I believe there are more ships from more countries coming into Bristol. Many of the vessels coming up the London river are mere coasters, indeed many of them never see blue ocean water at all. The cargoes coming into Bristol may hail from the East Indies, the Americas, Spain, and Africa. They are rich cargoes, rare cargoes, things that cannot be got in England (or across the Channel in France). If you had a mind to voyage, you could take your choice of vessels travelling to Constantinople, to Calcutta, even to California.

With all these rich cargoes changing hands, the men of business gather and their gold flows like rivers from the farthest corners of England and out across the seas. You have only to look at the fine houses being built around Bristol to see solid expression of the wealth of the city.

You know Bristol, you have travelled there and seen the fine buildings, but you travelled by land. Let me tell you how it appears to the mariner coming back to his home country after many years away. First, there is the Bristol Channel, one of the fiercest and busiest stretches of sea the world has to show. We came into the Channel inside of Lundy, leaving the island to port (to our left; port is left, starboard is right). Round the rocky coast of North Devon we sailed, and soon Wales was there to the north. The sea here is still clear and green, and smells fresh. With a good wind and fine weather, it can be a very fine trip. The hills of Exmoor stand out, and people and animals can be seen going about their business. After a shower of rain, the air can be so transparent that I have seen a shepherd and his dog walking out across the fields behind Porlock from a ship hard by the Welsh shore. Every valley has its church and houses, and sailors start to feel they are home again.

The nearer we sailed to Bristol, the muddier the water became. It is clear up as far as Porlock. After that it might lose some of its shine as it takes the river water from the Levels of Somerset, and then the very cloudy water of the Severn Estuary. By the time Flatholm and Steepholm are well behind you, Wales is fully as near to see as England and the Channel is becoming narrower and narrower.

Many sailors say the tides of the Bristol Channel are the highest in the world, and I do believe them. The mouth of the Channel, between Pembrokeshire and Devon, is wide and the tides are normal (although the currents run fast). You may imagine the tides in those parts being squeezed into the Channel as it gets narrower and narrower. The press of water is tightly confined as the tide reaches the Severn, and here it forms a remarkable natural phenomenon called the Bore. One spring tide I must journey up to see the Bore. I am told that the tide flowing up the river and meeting with the water coming down forms a huge wave which travels rapidly upstream, faster than a galloping horse. The local fishermen are well used to it and keep themselves and their boats well out of the water when it is due, for they would surely be swamped. I believe the Bore runs even up to Gloucester, though it is much smaller by then.

These powerful tides moving the sea up and down fifty feet or more leave a very sad shore at the mouth of the Avon River. There are mud banks and little else. It is a dismal entry to Bristol, to anchor off Avonmouth and wait for the pilot to take the ship up the river. The weather is usually foggy and even the clearest days seem to leave a haze over the land.

We waited for our pilot because every wise captain prefers to employ a man with local skills to enter port, especially a difficult entry like the Avon. When you think that the slightest mistake might bring disaster to the vessel and all aboard, it is understandable that the very best man should be employed.

Being passengers, Long John and his family were able to leave by cutter as we swung at anchor. It was two weary days before we had picked up our pilot and inched our way up the Clifton Gorge to Bristol. Then we had only to be paid our due, take our discharge, and we were free to swing down the gang-plank onto the busy Bristol Quay.

The Hunt Sets Out

We set our bags down on the quay and looked around us, wondering where we should go and what we should do to find Long John. We need not have worried. A dirty little boy trotted up, knuckled his forehead and recited in a rush, "Mr. Silver's compliments and if you would care to come to the sign of The Spyglass, he would be pleased to welcome you, an' he said you'd give me a 'alfpence, sir."

Following our tiny guide we pushed our way along the crowded waterfront, passing every class of merchantman in every class of readiness to sail. All around us, cargoes were being discharged into drays and lighters. Others were being swung into waiting holds. Wagons laden with ballast inched their way onto the wharf and returned laden with tuns of tobacco, or wine, or sugar, or any of the myriad products in which the men of Bristol trade and make their fortunes.

As with the cargoes, so with the men. All nations of the world were in the crowd, distinctive in face and dress. Swedes in profusion, Germans, Dutch, Spaniards, Moors, Africans, Levantines, all were there. Some from farther away, Chinese, Malays, Lascars, and Siamese.

Our guide turned sharply into a cobbled alley and we found before us The Spyglass, the sign of its name hanging over the door. We stepped down off the cobbles into the dark and smoky taproom, a long room sadly lit by the open door and a small window into the alley. We looked this way and that for Long John. We found him, not as we expected seated at one of the boards, but standing behind the bar and surveying the room with the air of a proprietor. He wore an old blue coat, and his smart hat had been replaced by a familiar salt-stained one.

"Welcome aboard, lads, welcome aboard!" he shouted. "Ashore at last. Here." He set two mugs and a jug on the counter. The grog tasted very good after our abstinence of the last few months.

We had a fund of all the questions we had kept in store since Long John surprised us on the Providence. He laughed at our confusion and the tales of our trials. Over our grog he told us that not only did he have a part share in the American Providence, but he also owned The Spyglass. In the two days since he had come ashore, Long John had set aside the fine clothes of a ship-owner and donned an inn-keeper's apron. He even looked the part. He was an old salt retired from the sea, keeping in touch with his mates by running a grog-shop. When we wanted to know how he had managed the miraculous transformation so quickly, he just winked and said, "Friends, lads, friends."

(I realise now that his 'friends' must have been the counting house that handled his shipping business and money. I wonder what they made of him. Did they think it strange that a wealthy man should want to become the owner and even the proprietor of a low grog-shop? Did they see the pirate lurking inside the fine clothes? Surely they must have done. Over the years I have noted how men of business, no matter how grand, think it no shame to close their eyes and debase themselves to the very gutter in search of a profit.)

Inn-keeper or not, Long John was as eager as we were to start on the business of finding Billy Bones. He had sent from the Americas asking his agents to obtain an inn for him. He had included a request for news of Billy Bones, a sailor recently landed from Charleston. His request may well have reached Bristol on the same ship as Billy.

"First things first!" Long John cried. "I'll go and rouse up the galley." He stumped up the stairs at the back of the tap-room, leaving us to look around and wonder. He did not stay away long, and returned followed by Mrs. Silver and her daughter bearing steaming sweet-smelling bowls of food.

"This is Dick and Caspar, m'dear," he introduced us. Mrs. Silver gave us a long look, but greeted us only with a shy smile. Long John was more welcoming. "Bring your grog over here, boys, and you can try the best victuals in Bristol."

We brought our mugs to the table and took the offered stools. The meal was magnificent, the best we had tasted for a long time. The bowls held white rice and a very fine and spicy chillo cooked by Mrs. Silver, redolent of the West Indies. What food that was, although I expect you would find it overwhelming, your tongue not being accustomed to the fiery peppers from those parts. After what we had been used to on board ship, it was milk and honey to us.

After Mrs. Silver had cleared the board and the three of us had settled to our grog and tobacco, Long John lent over the table and started on the news for which we had been waiting.

"As close as I can fathom it, he took the stage to Exeter. Leastways, it was either there or into Wales. And I'll lay it wasn't Billy that took off to Cardiff, not him. He must have been the one who went into Devon. He took the Falcon coach. Now we'll put you two aboard that same stage tomorrow, and you can ship to Exeter. When you get there, ask for your shipmate who got there about the twelveth of September." He paused to relight his pipe.

"I believe it'll be a lot easier than asking the same question in Bristol.

There's less people in Exeter for one thing. And for another, there's none too many sailors, neither." He stopped and thought for a while. "I wonder where the old fool's headed. He'll stay near the sea, I'll lay to that. But the sea's round every corner in those parts. He could be bound anywhere all the way to the Lizard, d--- him! An' we don't know but that he'll cross over to the other side, to the west. I suppose he'd still go to Exeter first. It's wilder over on the other side, what with the big winds off the Atlantic. I'll lay that he'll go that way, trying to hide himself in the wild places."

"What if we don't find where he's taken off to?"

"Ah, well. That's where the boot rubs, isn't it? 'Tis all well and good if you get there and someone tells you where to go looking. But if there ain't no news..." He grunted and took a pull at his grog.

"Now this is how it'll go, boys. You step off the stage, and go looking. Ask everyone you see. Don't be shy. Billy will have landed just the same as you, and he'll have gone off looking for somewhere to bed down. He won't be taking a room at the coaching inn, that's for certain. Not our Billy. He'll go looking for some grog-shop more his cut. But then again, if he'd wanted to ship out again, he'd have to go to an inn to get his place on a stage.

"You ask everyone. Start with the coaching inns. He'd get there soon after the twentieth of the month, so he could be remembered getting off. Or where he slept. Or where he went to board again. Most of the inns have a big book for passengers, so his name might just be in there, if he was using his own name. Just you stay in Exeter and keep asking around. An' if you don't find nothing, or you don't know where he went, write to me here. Write to me anyways, so as I knows where you'll be."

Long John paused and looked fiercely into our faces. "This is grave work, lads. You're the first of the crew here, and that speaks well of you. But you'll need an old head to stay afloat in this weather. D--- this leg, and I'd leave both of you here and ship out myself. But you'll have to do." He twisted in his seat and settled again.

"Now look you both. Do just as old John tells you, keep your rigging taut, and I'll see you have a soft berth when we ship out of here." He reached beneath his apron. "Here now. Here's ten guineas, five each. Keep out of the grog-shops and you can live like admirals. Send a letter to me every week to tell me where you are. Every week, mind. And I'll need to send you orders, so make sure I can find you.

I'll keep a weather eye out for the rest of the crew. When they drag their sorry hulks in here, I'll send them after you the moment you find Billy.

"Just find him. Don't let him know you're there, or he'll run again. Just spill your wind and lie low. Write your letter and you'll have help in a week if I have to come myself."

Again he stared into our faces. "You'll follow your orders, won't you lads? You'll do your duty by your old quartermaster?"

The intensity of his plea brought us up short, I began to feel a little of the reality of what I had set my hand to. We had seen Flint's treasure. We spoke often of chests of gold and jewellery, of kegs of silver covered in tarred canvas. Long John's urging gave it body. The chests had weight to them, and the silver pieces became something Caspar and I might have in our pockets. Grave work indeed.

Just then Mrs. Silver came down with mugs of chocolate. But I am cheating you. You have heard a little of your grandfather and I am sure you desire to know something of your grandmother.

At the time of which we speak, she was a mature woman of between thirty and forty years. She had lived a wandering life in the sea-ports of the West Indies, much of it as the wife of Long John. It must have been a difficult life, as is the life of all sailors' wives.

In England we are much surprised and a little curious when we meet a Negro (or Negress). Their skin colour seems strange, their facial character and tight curly hair unattractive. We are disposed to view them as servants or even slaves, and pay little attention to any true worth or accomplishment. This is perhaps natural. Ignorance breeds suspicion. I admit that when I first went to the West Indies, I did not like them and felt nothing but distaste for the black ladies, be they true Africans or Creoles.

However, young as I was, I rapidly became accustomed to the sight of black faces and to sailing with shipmates of all colours. In a short time I came to appreciate the pretty girls who lived in the Islands. They too were of all shades, from coal-black to the tawny colour of last year's honey. I became a subscriber to the opinion that, no matter what England has to offer in the way of finely bred ladies, they are left in the shade. The ports of the West Indies claim scarcely an inhabitant of pure blood, yet boast populations of handsome men and beautiful women in proportions far greater than Bristol or London.

But this is by way of a diversion, for I would not have you think poorly of your grandmother. She too was naturally handsome and had a graceful, unhurried carriage. In time I learnt she had a depth and force of character that rivalled Long John himself. She lacked learning of the bookish sort, being schooled by life alone. Not that her wisdom and experience was shared with us men, except perhaps with Long John. She said little to us that night or later. Her chosen companions were female, and it was only later that I saw how animated and playful she could become in their company.

What did she look like? Well she was very tall, almost as tall as Long John himself, with a long fine neck. Her skin had a colour rather like coffee to which a little milk has been added. She had delicate features and deep black eyes, so black that the iris seemed but an extension of the pupil. Her curly black hair was kept short and she habitually wore a length of some brightly coloured stuff wound around her head. Her lips were very dark, almost purple, which brought out the brilliant whiteness of her teeth. Also the pinkness of the tip of her tongue, which used to emerge when she was engaged in some particularly difficult piece of sewing or embroidery. Altogether a fine and beautiful woman, to whom you must be grateful for her beauty has passed on to you! That will suffice for the moment; I shall tell you more of her later, when she once again becomes important in our story.

Anyway, she brought us mugs of chocolate and sat with us a while. We exchanged stories of our different voyages aboard the American Providence, and Long John told us again how surprised he had been to find us there when he had boarded. Our surprise had been the greater for we had at least stayed in our station of ordinary sailors, whereas he had transformed himself into an owner, something we had never thought to see.

He chased us off early that night as we would need to wake with the dawn. Mrs. Silver showed us up to the big empty loft of The Spyglass where Long John had already slung two hammocks.

Picking up the Scent

Next morning saw Caspar and I seated high on the stage coach for Exeter, braving the late October weather. We were fortunate to have a still day with little wind to stir up the leaves, and no rain to make us outside passengers uncomfortable. We rode through a countryside at rest, everything prepared for the violence of winter and only waiting for it to arrive. If you are young, well-clothed (we had our sailor's clothes), and well-fed (we did not stint ourselves in that item), travelling outside a stage coach is a fine way to view England. From our lofty seats we could peer over the hedges and watch the cottages of the country people. The children passed by waving, and we waved back. Cattle ignored us. Horses might keep pace with us on their side of the hedge. It was a time of ploughing and burning, of gathering and storing against winter. The bleak Levels of Somerset swept by followed by bare, harvested apple orchards. Through the small, white-washed towns we clattered, on to Exeter.

Exeter is a fine town, as you know, and a more homely setting for the cathedral and its clergy is hard to imagine. We had not come there for the cathedral, however. We were looking for a sailor-man, an old man, tall, with a sea-chest, arrived from Bristol a month or more ago.

At the close of a grey afternoon our coach brought us to the door of The Sun, at the very top of Exeter's main street. This was the end of its journey, and all the passengers must dismount. Bundles, packets, trunks were all lowered to the pavements and as passengers gathered their luggage, the inn-keeper solicited them with offers of good food and feather mattresses. His attempt on our custom sounded half-hearted. The Sun was a fine establishment, prosperous and well-tended. Such a business did not grow from accommodating poor seafarers.

We, of course, were far more interested in him. He had probably met Billy coming off the stage, not so long before. Would Billy have made a mark on his memory? Given a good coat and hat, Captain Wm. Bones Esq. might have caught his eye. He might even have stayed a night or two. In any case, the man was far too busy with his guests at present. If we wanted to question him we would have to wait. The tap-room welcomed us and we sat by the fire warming our hands on mugs of mulled ale. From where we sat we could see travelling boxes and luggage being carried up to the chambers above. The inn-keeper hurried up and down the stairs, marshalling the porters and installing his visitors in their rooms. What a world of worries he had. This man insisted on his sending out for a good fresh salmon for dinner, for he would have no part of the steak and oyster

31

pie now cooking. That lady found her room impossible, lacking light near the looking glass. She would have to move rooms if nothing could be done about it. The people in the best room had a baby, and the infant's demands exceeded those of all the rest of the guests.

If only keeping people was as simple as keeping pigs or chickens, an inn-keeper's life would be a good deal more attractive.

For the moment, the tap-room stood empty and the girl charged with serving us had little to do. Under the pretence of replenishing the fire she stood, poker in hand, asking where we had come from, hungry for tales of strange things from over the seas. She was a pretty girl with a simple Devon accent, and you may be sure that we lost no time in spreading our feathers before her. We basked in her questions and exclamations of disbelief, and felt very fine fellows indeed. Behind us, the hubbub faded away as the guests settled in.

When I remembered why we were there, I asked if she had seen Billy. She had not. She would have remembered him, she said. She was always interested to hear tales from mariners. She knew all the captains and naval gentlemen who passed through regularly and sometimes gave her shells and such-like from foreign parts. We asked for the inn-keeper.

"You'll not find him now, my dears," she said, throwing her hands up. "'Tis his night for practicing with the bells. You'll soon hear him ringing away. Then he'll take himself off with the other ringers and get rotten drunk. We'll not see him before tomorrow." As an after-thought she added that she would not be standing there chattering if the inn-keeper was on the premises.

So, a wasted evening. Or partially wasted anyway. At least we knew that Billy had not stayed at The Sun. Our friend could not suggest where he might have gone. "I'm not from here, you know," she assured us seriously. "I'm from Crediton. All the bad places where the rough people do go are down by the river. I never go there, my dear. The things they do call out after you in the street. It's embarrassing, I can tell you. Your friend might've stayed down there, if he's that sort of man." She looked at us doubtfully. She was wondering if we were 'that sort of men'.

We pleaded that it was just a matter of expense. We could not afford to stay with her. "Oh, I see," she said innocently. "You're poor too. Don't you worry now. You just go down to the Widow Howard's in Mill Street. She'll take you in and she doesn't charge much. She cooks very nicely too." We made a show of remembering directions and assured her we would certainly visit good Mrs. Howard. We took our leave and headed down the High Street towards the river.

Our informant was right. The streets down the hill beyond the cathedral were much less prosperous. No one called out after us, of course, but there were plenty of sharp boys who might have made a country girl cry in vexation. We bought some hot chestnuts because they smelt so nice, and also because it gave us a chance to speak with the seller. What a blessing that Exeter is a smaller city than Bristol. He told us again and again that there were only two places a seafarer could go for a drink, a meal and a bed. One named Worthy's after its owner. The other was The White Hart. The chestnut man guessed Worthy's as the more likely place. Not only was it bigger, but it had a more popular tap-room. Apparently it had a name for wild carousing, a thing of which he approved.

We took our leave and set off to Worthy's, breaking open hot chestnuts as we went. The night was just about to close around the chestnut man when he called out to us. "Hey, listen, lads, the press is out and about. Keep a sharp eye for them." We shouted back our heart-felt thanks. How different our lives would be if the press-gang caught us.

Worthy's could only be found by asking. It had no such name outside. In fact a faded sign said 'Williams and Sons, Chandlers'. It was a narrow building of several storeys, tucked into an angle of the cobbled street. We stepped down into a narrow corridor and, passing through towards the back, found ourselves in a very large tap-room, its size belying the narrowness of the house frontage. Mr. Worthy stood behind the bar, looking completely out of place. A clerical figure with spectacles and dressed in old-fashioned black simplicity, he had something of the air of a Quaker about him. Not at all the man to be the proprietor of a roaring sailor's tavern.

He gave us a small room with a bed to share and, when we were uncertain as to how long we would stay, made us pay in advance for two nights, six pence a night each. While we had the chance we asked him about Billy, but in vain. As we followed him back down the crazy flight of stairs, we described Billy in detail, trying to strike a spark in his memory.

"It's no good, boys," he said over his shoulder. "Most every sailor in the West Country has taken a drink here at one time or another. I can't remember them. I shan't remember you next week."

"He's a big man," we repeated. "If he took his hat off, he's not got much hair. He likes to get drunk and sing."

"Get drunk and sing, eh?" He gave us a knowing look. "Get drunk and sing. Well, I believe he wouldn't be much of a sailor if he didn't do that on occasion. Everyone comes here to do that." And he left us for other customers.

Long John had told us to keep out of grog-shops, but in following Billy's trail we must frequent the places he would have done. So with easy consciences, we tucked ourselves into a corner and looked for victuals.

We soon noted that a good part of Worthy's success in business was due to his servants. He had realised that sailors would count being served by pretty girls a very fine thing, and by providing them, he brought sailors in by the dozen. He succeeded in making them feel like kings.

Several barmaids rushed in and out of the crowded tables bearing drinks and food to the boards. Of course, a rowdy house is no place for ladies, and the barmaids would hardly wear that name. Nor were they quiet and well brought up like our friend at The Sun. They were strong, forward girls with sharp tongues, easily able to return with interest the raillery of their customers.

We managed after a while to call one over to our table. The small, dark girl took our order for ale and pie, and disappeared. She returned bringing a loaded, succulent tray, fit to keep the damp autumn out of our bones. As she set the platters down I asked her name. She straightened up, ready to give a sharp retort but seeing I was not intending to intrude, answered politely enough.

"You may call me Jenny, sir," she said. "It'll be a fine change from some of the things we're called." She cast a pointed glance over her shoulder at the crowded room.

I was little used to questioning people, and hesitant to go on. But we had a man to find "Er...Jenny," I started. "There's something you could help me with."

Again she looked at us suspiciously, but softened as we described Billy. Then she shrugged. "You'll never find him by asking here. I could never remember a face from one day to the next, let alone a month ago."

In vain we pleaded. She did not recall Billy, and left as soon as she could. So there we were. Billy may have stayed in the house, but no one was likely to have noted him. We had no hint of him, nor did we have a sign-post to show our path.

First thing first, we set about our food. It is marvellous how a hungry stomach makes for lowness of spirit, and conversely, how a nourishing meal can set a man up. By the time our pie had gone, we had decided to try The White Hart that very night. If Billy had left a trace there, nothing would be gained by waiting for tomorrow.

The night was dark outside, no moon and little light coming from the crowded, leaning buildings. We started out down the cobbles, trying our best to avoid the puddles and rubbish in the street. It was very quiet. Not even a cat gave life to the deadness around us.

There occur in the affairs of men, very infrequently in a life-time, occasions when Providence seems to balance the whole course of a life on the edge of a knife. An inch, a second, a shilling more or less, and a man follows one road rather than another. Thus beggars may be made into great lords, future kind fathers into condemned felons, milk-maids into ladies. One of these occasions enveloped us on that dark street.

The first thing that happened was that my shoe-lace came undone. I crouched to tie it, and Caspar walked on whistling one of his old army marches. He had gone, I suppose, some ten yards in front of me when his whistling was cut off by several burly men jumping on him out of a narrow entry. As I stayed crouched in surprise, they quickly and efficiently secured his arms and immobilised him.

The press gang! I had yet to move when their leader ordered, "Thomas, get the other one." Then to Caspar, "No you don't, cully! King George has you now." As Caspar was cursing and attempting to break free, three or four of the sailors started towards me. Too late. With fear lending wings to my feet, I ran back up the road and into Worthy's like a rabbit fleeing into its burrow.

As I ran panting down the corridor to the tap-room, I met Jenny hurrying towards the kitchen with an empty tray. "Hey, watch yourself," she complained. "What's up with you?"

"The press gang's outside. They've taken Caspar."

Jenny set her tray against the wall and ran back to the tap-room with me on her heels. "Mr. Worthy," she called in a voice that set the whole room listening. "The press is outside and they've taken this boy's friend."

A silence fell on the room as each occupant thought of his own possible future. "Don't worry, lads," said Worthy. "They won't come in here. Now, boy, have you got any money?"

I did not understand his question. "How much?" I asked foolishly.

"Two guineas, maybe three," he said. "Speak up now. If you don't have it we shall have to have a whip round." Voices around the room murmured in assent, as the light slowly dawned on me. He was intending to ransom Caspar.

"No, no. I have it," I said, my hand going without thought to my purse.

"Don't give it to me yet," Worthy said. "Jenny, take one of the other girls and go after them. Where were they, boy?"

I stumbled out the directions with Jenny listening and she turned and ran from the room calling for a friend. Without pausing to take a shawl, they could be heard leaving at the front door.

"Now just you sit there, my lad," said Worthy. "Jenny will get him free, if anyone can. Give him a grog." I sat with my grog in my hand, still stunned by the rapidity with which events had unfolded. All the time a refrain ran through my head, 'saved by a shoe-lace, saved by a shoe-lace'. For if my shoe-lace had not come undone, I would that very night have started life as a sailor on one of His Majesty's great ships, and in all probability would have ended my days as such. Can you imagine what a difference that would have made? You would not have been at all, and I would not be caring for my parish. All for a shoe-lace.

Waiting for Jenny to return was a slow job, and it seemed as if more than an hour had passed before, chilled to the marrow, she came back to the tap-room. Silence fell as all around listened to her news. She told us that Caspar had been brought to the street outside, and that the men were waiting for their ransom. I followed her to the door. Worthy and I stood just inside while she went out with three of our precious guineas. Caspar stood between two sailors, large men with tarred pig-tails. He looked a little sheepish and held up his breeches with one hand. (It is the custom of the press gang to cut a man's belt and waistband to impede his running away.) Jenny stood to one side as the men released him, and then handed over what seemed to be two guineas.

I did not care. So pleased was I to see Caspar smiling again that I did not grudge her a guinea for her work. She had the grace to blush a little when I winked at her just to let her understand I knew. For the rest of our stay she was most attentive, especially to Caspar whom she treated much as a mother might.

In the tap-room Caspar was welcomed by all. Grog was sent to our table, another portion of pie, and strangers came to sit and take tobacco with us. Soon what could have been a very nasty adventure faded behind us. As the grog flowed freely, we began to relax rather more than Long John would have approved, so when some of the tables called for songs, we were ready to join in the merriment. Ballads and songs of the sea were tossed from table to table, the better singers leading us on until, inevitably, the turn came round to us.

As you know I am not much of a hand at singing, not even hymns, and Caspar was worse than I. However, it would have been grossly impolite not to have stood our turn and Caspar, still holding his breeches, finally stood and sang.

We had been a long time away from England and knew none of the new songs. Deserted by his old army tunes, Caspar turned to the shanty that we used at the capstan bars of the Walrus.

Fifteen men on a dead man's chest,
Yo-ho-ho and a bottle of rum.
Drink and the Devil has done for the rest
Yo-ho-ho and a bottle of rum

That terrible old song was unfamiliar to the rest of the room, but they soon picked up the refrain. Their yo-ho-ho's made the rafters ring. I was also doing my best to make the roof shake when I caught Worthy giving me a strange look.

When the singing had passed on, he came over. "Your shipmate," he asked, "The old man you were asking for, he'd know that song of yours? And he's a tall man with a cut here," marking his left cheek with his finger. "Old blue coat, pig-tail, a deal of white hair in his nose, am I right?"

We sat up sharply. Billy at last. "Yes, yes," we cried. "That's him. Do you know where he is?"

Worthy seemed not to hear. "I recall him, now. Sat right over there, he did. With…who was it now? Tom Brierly, I believe. No, there's no use looking for him. Tom's only here now and again. He's in and out of France mostly, and he was here only a couple of nights back. I believe your friend stayed here just one night. Came down here to sup, took his grog and sang that song, just as you did. Then he was off next day."

So we retired for the night with some sense of elation. At least we had found a step on the road Billy had taken. The night had taken its toll of our energy and we slept heavily.

The morning made things look worse rather than better. True, we had found a trace of Billy, but only of where he had been. Not of where he was bound, and that is what we needed to know. True we were safe and free rather than marching down to the sea with other pressed men, but our stock of guineas had taken a hard knock.

We ate breakfast in a corner of the tap-room, by a window looking out over the roof-tops towards the river. The room was quiet, the handful of guests being very subdued after the excesses of the night. Jenny was there again, bringing our bread and bacon, and we took a little of her time to ask again about Billy. She half remembered him now, but had not spoken to him. Caspar finally hit on the key to progress.

"Our shipmate," he said, "our Billy, probably had a sea-chest along with him. Now I don't see him carrying it all the way up into town to catch a stage-coach, nor even down to the river to take a boat. So what did he do? He must have found himself a porter, that's what. Now if you were sitting here and wanted a porter, what would you do? You'd ask Jenny, that's what."

We called Jenny over again and explained the idea. Her female curiosity was becoming aroused and she began to take a real interest in our quest. "There's only one man we use here, and that's John Thomas. I'll go for him."

She returned quickly with a small square man in tow. We invited him to sit with us and Jenny brought him a mug of small beer. At first he gave no help at all. No, he could not recall anyone of that stamp, and he was sure he would remember if he had moved a sea-chest. He did not take a sea-chest every day. Then he stopped and thought.

"When did you say it was? Now, then. That explains it. I was away visiting friends about that time," he said firmly.

Jenny shrieked with laughter. "He was taken drunk," she said. "And spent a week locked up. Visiting friends!" She was giggling with delight.

"That was it," John Thomas went on without embarrassment. "So I was. And my nephew Johnny was doing the work for me."

"I believe I remember now." Jenny was excited. "Go and get him quick. I'm sure he took a sea-chest one day along with a couple of empty herring kegs for Mr. Worthy."

"No call for that," said John Thomas, lifting his mug. "He's gone to Crediton with his Dad today. His Dad's a carter, you know. They left in the dark to be back today. I expect he'll be in before night. I'll send him round as soon as he's done the horses."

I've heard it said that the hardest thing for a hunter of wild animals to do is to wait. And as hunters of men, we found the same. We had before us a whole day with nothing to do. To stretch our legs, and let the girls get on with the cleaning, we walked up to the town. With time weighing heavily on us and no money to waste, we walked up one side of the main street staring into the shop windows. And then back down the other side. We looked at the empty cattle market. We walked around the cathedral close and even allowed our boredom to tempt us inside to look at the statues and tombs. This was the first time either of us had been inside a church for many years.

The grey weather relented a little in the afternoon. We walked beside the river in a weak sun, but that soon drew in and we were back early at Worthy's to wait for John Thomas's nephew. He came late, a tall spindly youth towering over his uncle. The pair of them sat down and asked if we were going to buy dinner. Even such information as we sought had a price it seemed. Jenny, herself more than a little curious as to what would come out, brought dinner for the four of us. Once it was safely on the table, John Thomas encouraged his nephew to talk.

"Right, boy. Tell the gentlemen what you remember." Then in an aside to us, "He remembers it all, you know. Speak up, boy."

The youth was tongue-tied. He turned red, he stared at the table, in his confusion he even put a piece of pie in his simple mouth. "He remembers it all," his uncle repeated. "Tell 'em where you took the chest, Johnny. To The Sun, wasn't it?" John Thomas nodded, and the boy took up the movement and nodded with him. "The gentleman was going to Barnstaple, wasn't he? With an old sea-chest?"

Again Johnny nodded, more vigorously this time, and still struggling with a mouth full of pie stated proudly, "He were a captain, he were." It was little enough, but he had told us all we needed to know. Billy had gone off to the north of Devon, a wild and sparsely populated part of the county where an old sea captain from foreign parts should be easy to find.

We retired that night full of elation at our success, and rose early to resume our pursuit. The first thing to do was to write to Long John. Having delivered the letter to The Sun to be carried to Bristol, (and fortunately avoiding the embarrassment of meeting our old girl friend and explaining why we had preferred Worthy's over Widow Howard's) we set out to walk to Barnstaple some fifty miles away.

I have not been to Barnstaple for many years now, but I hear the roads are not much improved. We walked not only to save money but also because such coaches as went that way travelled so slowly that we lost very little time. We were fortunate in the weather. Not only was there little wind but for once there were two days without the slightest shower of rain. With our jackets bundled over our shoulders, we followed wet and stony lanes up and down steep hills. Dark and twisted woods shadowed us, tall bare banks towered over us, and flocks of crows and starlings stalked the empty fields. We spent one night in a farmer's barn and the next under a rick in the corner of a field. Early the following morning, we reached the small market town of Barnstaple, sitting on the banks of the River Taw.

Feeling old hands at the game now, we started to enquire for Billy Bones. The first stop, as in Exeter, was the coaching inn, The Golden Fleece. And, as in Exeter, we had no luck at all. The inn-keeper had no interest in two sailors looking for an old ship-mate.

Sitting on Barnstaple quay we pondered our problem and watched the muddy Taw flow by. Of course, Billy had no orders to keep out of grog shops and a drink was probably the first thing he would seek after leaving the coach. We started to look for a grog shop. This small town had a choice of one, and we were lucky straight away. The barman not only remembered Billy but had helped him on his way.

"Your ship-mate, he didn't want to stay in Barnstaple. He wanted to stay in a small place, he said, and one where he could look out west when he liked. Said he wanted to keep an eye on the ships out of the Indies. I expect he wanted to be half afloat, which he will be because I sent him over to my cousin who keeps the Admiral Benbow at Welcombe Mouth. That's a small place, sure enough, and so near the sea he'll have it in bed with him when the gales blow."

Trying to conceal our excitement, we called for another round of grog and let the barman give us directions. It was easy enough. A fishing smack let us ride in comfort down the Taw, bump across the bar and beat over to Clovelly. This fishing village hangs onto its cliff-face like lichen to an old rock, weathering the worst storms the ocean can throw at it. There are no roads at all, only a succession of cobbled stairways leading in and out of the low, white-washed cottages and eventually to the flat ground above. Here we spent the night in a tavern, carefully obeying Long John's orders to keep out of the tap-room. We also had a care not to show any interest in Billy. Once we found out our course for the Admiral Benbow, it was off to bed and ready for an early start.

We were fortunate that Welcombe Mouth lies a little way off the Bude road, for we must not be seen by Billy. We made our walk from Clovelly in the blessed obscurity of a cold sea mist. It hid our passage from many of the country folk, but it is not possible to pass even the emptiest of Devon fields without becoming news for many tongues. When we had to, we gave out we were sailors heading for Plymouth by way of Bude. As the morning passed, so did the mist and we moved out to the cliff-top path to be less noticed.

The Admiral Benbow lay, as it does today, in one of those sharp little valleys that cut through the sea-cliffs and conduct small streams down to the sea. The steep valley sides were thick with gorse, dead bracken and brambles. The blackness of this cover hung over the cluster of white cottages below. The Admiral Benbow was the largest building, set on the seaward side of the hamlet, all sheltered from the rage of the sea by a bend in the valley. We left the footpath to shelter out of sight while we studied the hamlet. As we peered down through the gorse bushes, the noise of the farm-yards came up to us. Chickens chattered and scratched, and a young pup vainly tried to bar an old sow from entering a gateway. A steaming dung-cart ground up the muddy street on its way to the fields. We settled down for an uncomfortable wait.

We wished we might be in the Admiral Benbow, keeping warm in comfort instead of enduring the wet cold seeping into our bones. The inn lay quiet below us, its painted sign hardly moving in the wind, and we wondered where Billy might be. We did not have a long delay. Before we had finished our lunch of bread and cheese, the door of the inn opened and out stumped Billy Bones, all wrapped up in a short coat and carrying a spy-glass under his arm. Squaring his hat, he set off down the valley.

"He's looking old," Caspar whispered in my ear. It was true. Billy looked a little bent, and perhaps his step was short and stiff. "The old devil will turn up his toes before we can get hold of him."

I was more interested in leaving our hiding place as quickly as possible and getting away from the long spy-glass Billy carried. When he passed under some trees we drew back from the valley and, out of sight of the village, made for the road. Here we conferred. We had to get word back to Long John, and we had to keep an eye on Billy. Watching him too closely would only scare him into running again, but we did not want to lose him. If he did run, he might go south towards Bude, or may be north to Bideford and Barnstaple. He might ship out on a coaster, but Bude would be the handiest place for that anyway. We decided that Caspar would carry on to Bude as we had intended, but I would go back to Bideford until Long John sent help. If Billy took the road north or south, we would be waiting for him.

Watching and Waiting

It is a tedious business indeed to wait a week or more with no duty to perform, and Bideford quay is cold in winter. The dark grey cobblestones seemed to forever glisten in the fading light of the year, swept clean by the wind and rain rushing in from the ocean. A few coasters rode up the Torridge, bringing cargoes of coal and wheat, and drifted out again when the weather allowed loaded with clay or timber or wool. The fishermen did little fishing at this time of year, taking just enough to keep their families with fresh fish. Their major work was the long business of overhauling the boats and their gear, stripping old paint and replacing rotted planking, readying their craft for the next year. The next year was still a long way off and if the weather turned bad, they were as likely to stay at home as they were to work. The rush would not really start until February had passed.

I took lodgings with a washerwoman, the widow of a fisherman, who was glad to earn a little extra to keep her children. At least I had shelter and food, but the days were very long. Also my money would not last forever and I needed work to eke it out. By rising before dawn, I soon found work unloading boats, helping mend nets and cordage, and getting the little fishing vessels ready for sea again. Turning my hand to some carpentry and painting kept me busy by the river, where I could observe all that passed.

My efforts brought little money but a great deal of pleasant conversation with the inhabitants of the quayside. I gave out that I was waiting for a ship-mate, my excuse for watching everything that passed over or under Bideford Bridge. I had no idea how help would arrive, by land or sea, but I confidently expected one day to see a crowd of my ship-mates come marching down the quay.

The winter days drew in and the fishermen spent more time ashore painting and mending. Christmas gusted in on a fine gale and was soon gone. I had written to Long John and now received a cheery letter in his bold hand bidding me wait a little longer and to write again should I need anything. The New Year too rode in on a wild storm.

One grey and windy afternoon, trying to keep the chill out of my bones, I walked across Bideford Bridge. The tide was out and the Torridge had shrunk to a dark runnel gurgling through the mud between the great piers. A blind beggar wrapped in a ragged grey coat came tapping towards me.

As he approached, he was whistling. I recall thinking how strange that such a creature, in such a place, should be whistling the Walrus's old song 'Fifteen Men'. Then I recognised him. It was Pew.

"Can you spare a ha'penny for a blind old man, young fellow? I can tell you're a fine young man by the way you walk, you know. Spare a ha'penny for a poor old sailor that's lost the very light from his eyes." He came up to me and as I started to name him again he hissed, "Shut up, you young fool!" and started to whine again. "Help a poor old man, young sir."

As I fumbled in my pocket, Pew whispered, "Start out on the Bude road at eight o'clock tomorrow, and I'll wait for you on the road." Then he set off again. "A whole penny. Thank'ee, young sir, you're a fine young gentleman and no mistake. Thank'ee, sir." And he tapped away. With difficulty I collected my wits and continued across the bridge. Long John had sent Blind Pew to help.

Next morning found me marching out on the Bude road, meeting carts and farmer's wives with their pack-ponies coming to market, searching for the blind beggar. I walked a long way looking for Blind Pew and was on the point of turning back and looking again when I saw him ahead, climbing slowly up a hill.

"Well then, Dick," he said as I came up to him. "Are you glad to see your old ship-mate? Are we steering the right course, boy? I've come to keelhaul Billy Bones, I have. Long John wants me to pass on our compliments to him." Pew had been well accustomed to his own company, since he lost his sight, and often held long discussions with himself. Even in conversation he frequently managed both sides of a discussion single-handedly.

I wanted to know where the others were, and just what Long John thought two boys and a blind beggar might do to Billy while he was safely tucked away in the Admiral Benbow. Even if Pew had his eyes back, we could hardly wrest the map from him without bringing the whole countryside out against us. But those were not Pew's orders at all.

"Oh yes," he said, "Long John's compliments to you, Billy, and would you be pleased to hand over that chart? Just hand it over nice and peaceful like, and he'll forget all about the sorry dance you've led him. You can beach yourself here and no questions. But if it don't please you to hand it over..."

Pew had set out with Black Dog to meet us. If Black Dog was the eyes and legs of the expedition, then Pew was the brain. He had sent Black Dog on to Bude to meet Caspar and return to Welcombe Mouth. If all went well, he would talk to Billy at the Admiral Benbow today. Long John had sent a message or, more exactly, a simple threat. If Billy parted with the chart peacefully, he might rest undisturbed in his retreat. If he tried to keep it, we would take it from his dead body.

Long John had written me a kind letter that started with compliments and went on to repeat Pew's orders. If Billy tried to run again, we were to catch him in the open and take the map from him by force. If he stayed at the inn, we were to lie up and wait for Long John. The letter was quite clear; lie up somewhere near the inn, close enough for word of our presence to get to Billy. A few days of waiting for us to strike might scare him into volunteering the map.

By the time Pew and I arrived on the deep road running towards the village, Black Dog had already met Billy. He was waiting for us beside the road, looking pale and angry. For a little time all we could only get oaths and imprecations from him, but eventually the tale of the meeting emerged much as Livesey has told it. Billy and Black Dog sat down to drink together, and Black Dog questioned Billy about the chart. At first he denied any knowledge of it and would talk only of his old ship-mates and his voyages with Flint. Then, dreaming aloud, he talked of fitting out a fishing boat or a coaster and going back to search for Flint's treasure. In his wandering, he let slip that he knew the latitude and longitude of the island, and realised he had given himself away. Straight away, he lost his temper and attacked Black Dog. "Chased me right out of the inn, he did," complained Black Dog. "Near split me in two with his cutlass, and me not able to stand and spit him, or we'd have lost the chart for good."

Black Dog led us up the side of the valley to where Caspar was watching the inn. Here, with our backs to an old thorn, we could peep over the dead bracken and brambles at the Admiral Benbow and the village. A pretty place in summer, no doubt, but in January the dead grass on the bank was wet and there was mud underfoot. The thorn gave no shelter from the west wind with its driving rain. We grew heartily sick of the view from that hill-side over the following wintry days.

We set up camp in a steep coppice a short way up the valley from the village. We had company. A couple of gypsy families were also camped there. Pew sent Caspar back to Bude for a tarpaulin next day, and we lay on the brush wood the gypsies gave us.

They led a bleak existence in winter. A local farmer had rented the coppice to them, and they were engaged in making thatching spars and clothes pegs. Not every day, of course. There is hardly a market for spars at that time of year. When the weather was too bad, they just sat crowded in one of the tents, talking and telling stories. They spoke their own language amongst themselves, but when we visited they swapped stories with us in English.

I own to sharing the popular prejudices against gypsies. Chickens and worse are stolen where they pass by. They are a dirty lot, living close to the ground, and it is true that the men in particular will go a long way to avoid doing a hard day's work. But set against that, they are wonderfully good company with a fund of talk and sayings that lodge in your memory for years. I cannot say that we stole any babies. Nor did we eat any hedgehogs (there being none around in winter.) We did dine several times on hare and pheasant that were not legally purchased, and I will not deny there were stolen turnips along with them.

The young children, boys and girls, were very forward in an innocent sort of way, and it was through one of them, called Lizzy, that I had my fortune read. She was, I suppose, about ten years of age, a nut-brown complexion kept passably clean, and had long black wavy hair. She wore gold rings in her ears and had black eyes that promised to be the ruin of men in a few years time. She drew me to her grandmother, the most respected member of the band, to have my fortune told.

If Grandmother had looked like her granddaughter, it must have been many years before. Now she looked little, very small in fact, and rather bent. Her white hair was wrapped within a patterned brown headscarf. She had no rings in her ears but a gold cross hung about her neck, an incongruous ornament for a fortune-teller. Her face was much creased, with a fierce nose jutting out of the wrinkles. Only in her eyes could you recognise her granddaughter, bright, black and piercing.

She insisted on silver in the traditional way, saying that a free fortune was no fortune at all. I gave her a penny that she hid beneath her shawl. Then she led me to the tent door-way, needing light by which to see my palm. She sat on a stool and I was forced to kneel at her feet. My friend stood at her shoulder where she could see all that passed and look into my face.

First the old lady took both my hands in hers and examined the backs of them. Then she turned them over and drawing them closer to her face studied them slowly. Gruffly she told me to look into her eyes. She stared straight at me. She was looking, so it seemed, deep down inside me. Then closing her eyes, her fingers traced my palms one after the other.

"You're a sailor man, a travelling man. You've travelled early, you'll travel soon, and you'll travel late. You'll have silver in your hands early and be a poor man. You'll have little in them late and be a rich one."

"There's a black-haired lady early," (here the girl sighed), "but not late. And another, black-haired girl late, but not early."

She stopped and started to hum to herself; and in a more normal voice,

"There's black work ahead, very black. So black that you'll be wearing black for many a year. 'Tis strange that a young man should meddle with such things. It wouldn't serve, but that's what the voices say. You'll find a treasure you haven't looked to find." She started to hum again.

"A treasure, for sure. I hope you'll recognise it when it comes. For you'll lose it, certain as anything. You'll find it and lose it. 'Tis strange..."

Still with eyes closed, she reached up to my head - a hand on either side, with a horny thumb pressed into each temple. "Hold still," she hissed as I started to pull away, "Put your hands on mine, girl, and feel what you feel. You won't find a fortune like this every day." The girl moved behind me and I could feel her against my back as she added a light pressure to her grandmother's hands. "What do you feel, girl? Do you see the break? Do you see the change in his life?"

Her voice went back to the sing-song tone, "What you are now, you'll not be then. What you will be then, you couldn't be now. You're a black man in a white shirt now, but you'll be a white man in a black shirt then."

Suddenly she opened her eyes and let me free. The girl put her hands on my shoulders as the old lady looked at me again. "A rare fate, young man," she whispered. "But follow it, boy. There's nothing you can do to change it now. Follow it, and at least you'll live through it. But you'll be a very different man the next time you pass this way." She rose and went back into the tent. Just then Pew called me and I made my way up to our eyrie with a long watch to ponder on what had passed.

The three of us with eyes took turn and turn about out on the hillside while Pew waited in the damp and miserable coppice for us. Sometimes he would walk out to beg, although not from the village, and in this way we heard what was happening at the inn. We heard of Billy's seizure after Black Dog's visit, and of Hawkins's father's illness, as well as a lot of village gossip about people we never knew.

Black Dog, in charge of our party, had a man on watch all the day-light hours. Caspar and I would have left it alone once Pew had word of Billy's state of health, but Black Dog said that Long John would hang us all if he came and found no one on watch.

We became familiar with the sight of all the village people and knew who was married to whom, who owned the children and chickens. We had no sight of Billy but the Doctor (that was Livesey, whom we were to know better) came and went several times. Eventually the priest came late one afternoon and we heartily wished his concern was with Hawkins's father and not with our quarry.

The next day came sunny and warm, with a promise of primroses to join the snowdrops in our coppice. There was a great to-do at the inn with many people coming and going, and late in the morning Hawkins's father was carried out in his coffin and laid on a farm cart. The whole village followed the bier up the valley towards the church.

I was just wondering whether to leave my post and tell Black Dog that the inn was probably deserted when dropping down from the cliff path into the valley came three figures, indisputably sailors. Israel Hands, O'Brien and George Merry. They strolled past the front of the inn, looking at first this sight then another, as if they were walking out after Sunday lunch. They made their way up the valley towards our coppice. I admit to an error here. If I had had the wit to rush down now and lead the others to the inn, we could have taken the chart and been gone before the village returned. However, it was not to be and you may be sure I thought bitterly of it afterwards. In the end, everything turned out for the best for the finding of the chart was the making of Hawkins.

My time dragged on and on. I wanted to go down below and greet my ship-mates but duty of a sort kept me at my station. People started to come back from the church, and Hawkins with his mother returned to the Admiral Benbow. The village came back to life and human noises mingled with those of the animals. I fretted beneath the thorn bush. It was long past the hour for my relief.

Suddenly a black shadow appeared through the bushes beside the road below. I made out Pew, tapping his way slowly through the village towards the inn. As he passed its door, he seemed to sense where he was and turned and spoke to someone unseen. He disappeared inside. After a minute or maybe two, he flew out again. His rags flying about him and with his staff under his arm, he tumbled down the steps and ran a few steps into the road. Stretching his staff far out in front of him, he ran as fast as he dared away from the inn, slowing to a walk only when he reached the houses of the village.

Israel and Caspar came up soon afterwards and I learnt the meaning of what I had seen. Pew had carried the Black Spot to Billy, and Billy still had enough power in him to make his displeasure felt. (The Black Spot is a rather grand name for a sort of round-robin but, pirates having little learning, the spot in the middle has more significance to them than their names around the edge.)

Bread and broth waited for me in the coppice, and a welcome from George and O'Brien. The older men were arguing over what should be done next. Their main difficulty was Long John, waiting aboard a lugger in Kitts Hole nearby. He could not wait there long for the weather would surely turn that wicked coast into a lee shore soon. Black Dog was all for facing up to Billy that afternoon.

"Let's go in and cut him out," he said. "I'm sick of this place. Let's do something and get out of this d----d wood."

Pew sneered. "That's all you can offer, is it? You know there's revenue men hereabouts. We'd have King George himself chasing us if we break in there. We'll have to smoke him out. Once he's on the open road, nobody'll care a wink for him, nor us neither."

"Well, that's fine and dandy," said Israel, "but how are we going to go about it? Billy ain't half mad enough to set sail with us waiting just over the bar. And Long John can't wait forever where he is. We'll have to get to Billy fast, before the weather turns."

So it was we agreed to wager all on the events of that night. If we could get the chart, we would make our fortunes. If not, our attempt would raise such commotion that we would no longer be able to stay. Caspar and I were greatly relieved to hear that. Come what may, we had just spent our last day in that cold and windy valley.

We used the remaining day-light to sharpen our knives and get ready to leave. George Merry went off to warn Long John and came back as the light failed. All along we did not know that Pew's little scrap of paper, the Black Spot, had finally carried off Billy Bones, doing what cutlass and cannon had failed to do for so long.

Darkness came and the frost crept through our clothes as we huddled around the fire. The quiet of the grave settled on the village and our coppice.

The moon rose and we moved out of our cover. A white mist had filled the valley bottom and blanketed the village. For a while it swirled about our legs then it swallowed us up. A small piece of the world a few yards across travelled with us down the road. Beyond that we could see and hear nothing. The damp and piercing cold had driven even the dogs inside and the houses passed by in unnatural silence. As we left the village, we stopped and I went on alone.

The road felt strange and empty. Long after I had expected it, there was still no sign of the inn. Doubts and fears crept around me in the mist and I was near to turning back when I came first to an outhouse and then the inn itself, silent and dark. I tried the latch of the front door. It was locked.

What a hand Providence chose to take in our affairs at this

moment. In the few minutes it took for me to hurry back to the others, Hawkins and his mother slipped away. And instead of walking straight into our oncoming band, the same hand led them to hide in a culvert a stone's throw from the inn. How the Good Lord protects the innocent!

Pew stood back in the road while we rushed the inn front and back. We found the front door unlocked, and I was cursed for a fool and a coward. We blundered in, scattering the benches. Our lantern showed an empty tap-room and the shrunken figure of Billy Bones stretched out on the floor. "He's been done. He's dead," someone shouted to Pew outside.

"Search him," shouted Pew. "Look in his boots, his hat. And find his chest."

"It's no good, Pew," called Black Dog, even as he was struggling with Billy's boots. "He's been done already. His pockets is out and his coat's been gone through."

I picked up his hat that lay in a corner. Empty, but I put it on all the same. His cutlass lay beneath the table half out of its scabbard. I took that too, and started up stairs. A lantern burned in Billy's room. His chest had been dragged out and the contents scattered about. There was not much— a little clothing, a worn pistol wrapped in an oily cloth. Billy's spy-glass lay thrown aside with his oil-skin jacket. His best hat had been trodden on. It too was empty.

We peered into the chest. There was nowhere the chart could be concealed. George smashed the window and called down to Pew. "It's gone, Pew. Someone's been through the chest. It must be that boy or his mother. There's nothing here."

"Find 'em," Pew raged. "They're hiding. Look out round the back. Or the beach. Look on the beach." Israel and Black Dog, calmer than the rest of us, started to go through the other rooms. I rushed out to the back of the house with the others. The mist had lifted a little and I could clearly see Pew cursing and shouting in the middle of the road.

"Round the back, you swabs. George, get down to the strand. Find those thieving weevils and slit 'em. What've you got?" Black Dog was coming out of the inn.

"They've gone." He spat to one side. "And now we'll have the village down on us. D---- 'em." Pew would have none of his resignation. He still screamed at us and sent us here and there.

"Cut and run, Pew," Black Dog shouted at him, and stopped short as a piercing whistle came from the direction of the village. "That's Caspar! I'm off," and he started to run along the road towards the sea.

Pew became so enraged he must have been on the verge of a seizure himself. Oaths and curses poured out of him. The rest of us hesitated then a second whistle from Caspar made up our minds and we fled. Much to our shame we left Blind Pew behind.

As we ran up the hill after Black Dog, we could hear him calling for us. Then his shouts died in a thunder of hooves.

Following the Chart

We felt a chastened band when we tumbled aboard Long John's lugger that night and set sail for Bristol. Look where all our effort and scheming of the past months had led us. The chart had gone, the county was raised against us and Pew had been taken or worse. Surely after no more than a few questions from the excise men, Pew would lead them to our door in Bristol. Our long journey from Savannah had come to naught, and our very lives lay in jeopardy.

Long John was in the cabin with Israel Hands. He had poured defamations and curses over us when we arrived empty handed, but once the storm was over he had laughed and welcomed Caspar and me warmly. Then he had set the two of us on watch and Caspar had the tiller. The sea was grey and smooth. With a quavering breeze on our quarter we rolled gently as we crossed the swell. The heave of the deck and the flap and slap of the rigging all felt very fine after so long ashore. And the smell too, not just of the fresh sea but also the tar and fishy smells of the lugger itself.

Israel came on deck. "Rouse 'em up, Dick. We're going ashore." I went below to shake hammocks.

Back on deck, Long John had the lead going and had taken the tiller himself. We stood into a rocky cove to drop anchor. The lugger towed her dory astern and it was a matter of moments to pull her up. Israel and I were rowed ashore and left on the ocean beach to stumble over ice-rimed boulders to firm ground. Behind us, the lugger was already laying a silver moon-lit wake across the sea as it sailed north for Bristol.

Israel and I wrestled with the problem of finding a way up onto the cliffs. People in those parts do not live too close to the sea. The Atlantic weather is altogether too wild, and the beaches too rocky to use. When they come down to the sea to look for shellfish, or to launch a fishing boat, they use winding earth paths through the brambles and stunted thorn bushes. All fairly obvious by daylight but desperately difficult to find at night. Added to that, we must pass no houses. With the excise out and searching, we did not wish to be associated with the attack on the Admiral Benbow.

Where we had landed I do not know. I expect we were somewhere in the region of Hartland. Anyway, by the time we reached the Bude road, muddy and scratched, a greyness had come into the eastern sky. We headed south, eager to return to our coppice at Welcombe Mouth. We were the first folk out and about on the road, and judging by the way the weather had started to come in off the sea, there would not be many people out that day.

We reached our goal about the time our gypsy friends were preparing breakfast. The young girl Lizzie sat beneath our tarpaulin, nursing a baby brother. Her grandmother obviously suspected we were not going to return and had already made a claim of possession. But she was happy enough to see us and brought breakfast, bread and turnip soup with more than a hint of pheasant.

So why did we go back? Well, look at your grandfather's spirit. He knew we had lost the chart, probably with no chance of recovering it, but he was not going to give up any chance of reaching the treasure. He wanted to know who had the chart, and how he could at least get a look at it. To that end he had sent Israel, who was still unknown in the area, to make enquiries. I went as a guide.

"I didn't look to see you people again," said the old lady, watching her granddaughter serve our portions. "I hear there was a right set-to in the village last night." She looked hard at me and I am sure I wriggled under her sharp eye. Israel was a better horse trader.

"Is that right?" he asked, sounding naturally innocent. "Did you hear what it was all about?"

"No, I did not," said out hostess tartly, "but I will shortly, when Lizzie goes down to get some eggs. I must have my eggs, and I'll have some news along with them." She started to sing to herself in a soft, wavering voice.

"So little Lizzie is going down to the village," Israel addressed my little friend. "Now if you was to come by any news, any interesting news, I believe I might come by a farthing for you." The girl pouted at him and said nothing.

"Get on with you." Israel laughed at her. "A whole farthing and that's not enough for you? Very well, a ha'penny and no more. But it will have to be interesting news for all that."

The girl ran off for a basket while her grandmother fussed about at the back of her tent. "Here you are, Lizzie," we heard her saying. "Three coney skins and two dozen pegs."

"Oh, Gran," Lizzie pleaded. "Nobody will take nothing here. Let me buy the eggs."

"You lazy jade, come here and get these. She thinks money grows in the fields like mushrooms," she muttered half to herself and half to us. The girl resigned herself and put the skins and the pegs in her basket. The old lady shouted to her as she started down to the road below. "Mind you get at least four for each of them skins! I tanned them proper and they're nice and soft."

The bad weather had reached us now, and we could hear the wind threshing the tree-tops. Where we had camped near the valley bottom, we felt little wind and we had only the inconvenience of the rain dripping from the trees. It was a day for sitting by the fire, keeping warm and telling stories.

I sat by the door of Grandmother's tent and watched for Lizzie. She came after a long wait, hurrying up the slippery path with her basket under her cape. She rushed inside and, leaving the sodden cape at the door, claimed a place close to the fire.

"What did you bring, my girl?" asked Grandmother, rooting through the basket, "How many eggs is that? What! Just ten? You let my coney skins go for just ten eggs?"

The girl was unconcerned and just giggled. "No, Gran. Only two of them. Two skins and two dozen pegs. I did well, didn't I?"

The old lady rooted again and retrieved the stray skin. "So you did, so you did. Now you may have some tea to warm you up." Drawing a can up from somewhere behind her, she threw a handful of leaves into a small pot and put it on the fire. "Now then. What did you hear?"

Seeing she had our full attention, Lizzie was not disposed to let her news go lightly. "I went to Mrs. Hancock."

"I know," said Grandmother. "You went to see young William."

"No, I didn't, Gran." Lizzie blushed. "He wasn't there anyway."

"So you were looking for him then?"

"No, I wasn't. I was looking for Mrs. Hancock for the eggs. And she wanted the coney skins. I made her take the pegs too."

"Hmm. I don't care about the pegs. Your father made them. But I tanned them skins. What does she want with them?"

"She's going to make slippers for the new baby. He's ever so nice, with blue eyes."

"Yes, yes. Don't you get interested in babies yet, there's plenty of time for that. Now, what did you hear?"

"Mrs. Hancock said there were highwaymen at the Admiral Benbow last night."

Grandmother looked sharply at us. "Highwaymen, eh? And what were they doing there?"

"They robbed the inn. They took away all Mrs. Hawkins's money and jewellery. And they broke the chairs and then they went off to Bude."

"What did they do to Mrs. Hawkins?"

"She wasn't there. She'd run away with Jim, and she was hiding in a ditch under the road. She says she could hear the highwaymen talking just two yards away, but they didn't see her. She said they wanted to cut her

53

throat."

Grandmother thought about the news. "Highwaymen, you say. Now the Admiral Benbow's a fair way from any highway. And they'd be hungry men indeed if they had to rely on Madam Hawkins's jewellery box for a living. What else did you hear?"

Lizzie let go another bit of news. "The old captain's dead. Mrs. Hawkins said he had another stroke yesterday, before the highwaymen came. She says it's the best thing that came out of a black day."

"Highwaymen." Grandmother was still gnawing at the idea, like a dog at a bone. "Now if you were to say they were sea-faring highwaymen, that might fit with the old captain, mightn't it?" She looked at Israel but said nothing. "What else did you hear, girl?"

"Jim Hawkins went with the Doctor to Mr. Trelawney's house. Mrs. Hawkins said the old captain gave him a treasure map before he died, and the Squire wanted it. He went there with the excise men."

"The excise men as well? Now there's a thing. You don't get excise men without there being smugglers. And the Admiral Benbow might be a handy place for smugglers. Call your highwaymen smugglers and I'll start to believe you. What else, girl? You're hiding something."

"The blind man's dead. The excise men ran him down outside the inn."

Lizzie seemed no more concerned about this piece of news than the rest of her story, for all that Pew had been living with us. I suppose he was not an easy man to love.

"Pew's dead?" Israel started out of his quietness. "Pew that was here along of Dick?"

"He's dead," confirmed Lizzie, "And they'll be burying him this afternoon."

"You stupid hussy!" scolded Grandmother. "Why didn't you tell us straight out?" She turned to Israel. "Now, my boy, I don't know what you were all about last night, nor why you came here. Let the King take care of his own duties, I say. But sure as eggs are eggs, we shall have a visit from the excise. Once they find out that Pew was staying here, they'll be up here looking around.

"You'd better be on your way now, no time to lose. Get back up the hill and go back to where you came from."

"But what about the chart?" I blundered in.

"The chart?" Grandmother seized on my concern as quick as a terrier on a rat. "Oh-ho! So the Squire has your chart and you can't do without it. Am I right? That's why you came back. Israel Hands, getting the truth out of you is like getting blood out of an oak tree. And how can your friends help you if you don't let on what you're about?

"Now let me think." She closed her eyes and seemed to be chewing over ideas with her old gums. "I know. Get back up the hill where they won't see you, and up to the Bude road. Go straight across from the Welcombe road and about a mile and a half in. You'll come to another wood much like this one. It drops off on your left down into a valley. Down there at the bottom you'll find my cousin Emmy.

"She stays there more or less permanent. She's stopped travelling now. You just tell her that Cousin Elspeth sent you, but don't say no more. The village folk visit her, you see. She makes them up cures and such like, so there's always folk coming round to cure a sick cow or a broken heart. If you talk too much, the whole countryside will hear of it within the day."

The old lady thought a little more. "I believe you'd better take your tarpaulin with you, but I shall think better of you if you leave it for me when you move on. I'll send Lizzie after you with news, if there is any. She seems to have a yen for Dick here."

"Oh, Gran, don't!" Lizzie was blushing. She looked to run out of the tent as we laughed at her, but the rain held her back.

"Now, get on with you," said the old lady abruptly. "They may come anytime."

Leaving Pew to be buried in a pauper's grave by the Parish, we scrambled up through the wood taking turns with the sodden tarpaulin. It was not a long walk, but the wind blew cold and miserable. It drove blasts of rain across the fields and I blessed my good sea-faring oil-skins, a gift from the Providence (what a long time ago that seemed!)

We found Cousin Emmy easily. The paths through the wood all converged towards the bottom of the hill. There, under the beech trees, stood a small hovel, just as the charcoal burners use, with a wisp of smoke trickling out of its disorderly black thatch. Also trickling out was the sound of a thin, cracked old voice singing, and singing in a strange language.

"Ho there!" called Israel as we approached. "Is that Cousin Emmy there?"

The singing stopped. "I believe it might be. But who would be wanting her?"

"Cousin Elspeth sent us."

"Did she indeed? If she sent you here, she must be trying to physic you or hide you and you don't sound like you need no physicking. Is that true, or isn't it?" From the shadows of the hovel's interior came a remarkable little woman. A little bent, and brown as a nut, she wore heavy green skirts and a thick black shawl wrapped tightly round her. No hat covered her straggly grey hair, and gold ear-rings peeped out from under it. I believe

55

she would have looked everyone's vision of a witch, but for her clear eye and the smile waiting to break over her creased face.

"Oh, great big men!" she said with surprise. "And where am I meant to put you? And what will you eat? Acorns?"

We felt abashed. "Er, we have a tarpaulin," I mumbled.

"So you have. So you have. And you may pitch it there." She waved us to the next beech tree. "But do you have any pennies? Without pennies you'll have a very light supper." Israel hastily offered sixpence. "Oh, men of wealth and fashion. Well, we'll dine well enough on that. And how long might you be staying?"

There was something about Cousin Emmy that commanded a great deal of respect, and for once Israel had his wings clipped. "We'll be here maybe a week, ma'am, if you please."

Cousin Emmy looked at us carefully. "Ma'am, eh? I believe I shall like you after all. But that's enough of that. Call me Emmy, without the fancy handle, that'll do. And don't think you'll be living like lords on sixpence a week, neither."

As Israel fumbled in his pocket for more money she stopped him. "No, no. Not now. I shall ask you when I need it. Now come along inside and warm up. You can look to your tarpaulin when the rain lets up. If it's going to, before the day goes."

As we huddled around the small fire, she got on with making some pan-bread to feed us. We had obviously come to an inn of some distinction.

The next few days we spent helping out with household work. We scoured the woods for dead branches (we were not allowed to touch any green timber.) The wood pile we made would certainly see Emmy through the rest of the winter. We dug a new privy and laid stepping stones across the muddy places in her paths. Stone steps down to the stream made fetching water a good deal easier for our hostess and kept us warm and busy during the building of them.

Emmy brought us food from the village, mostly potatoes and turnips in truth, but January is a hungry time of year. It seemed the winter was thinking to leave, and warmer weather brought on the first of the primroses, so our little forest was not a bad place to be waiting in.

Lizzie visited us on our second day with Emmy. She brought news that the very fields were buzzing with the story of Flint's chart. It seemed the Squire, Mr. Trelawney, had seized upon it and had determined to use it himself and make his fortune. Next day I walked to Bideford to send to Long John the information we had gathered so far.

Several days later Elspeth came herself with little Lizzie for a visit. The spring sun dappled through the bare branches around us as we sat at a small fire, and talked of this and that. Elspeth circled round and round the subject of Flint's chart. She was trying to get us to talk of the treasure and how we came by knowledge of it. I kept my mouth shut and Israel fended her off, continually trying to change the subject of our talk. In the end curiosity got the better of subtlety and she attacked us head-on.

"Israel Hands, I know you for the most cross-grained, ungrateful son of a pig-gelder with more than one foot on dry land! Here am I doing my best to help you along, and you'll not give the smallest taste of what you're after. Well, if that's your fancy, you can ask elsewhere for the latest news!" Leaving this tantalising hint hanging in the air, she started to fumble in her pocket and came out with the blackened stump of a pipe. After some more fumbling, she made a show of filling it and reached for a spill from the fire to light it.

"Elspeth, my dear," said Israel, "Don't take on so. You told us yourself to keep mum. We don't want half the kingdom following us around."

Elspeth said nothing but drew deeply on her pipe to get it well alight. She might not have heard. Emmy watched them both with amusement, sure of the outcome.

"Come on, Elspeth," cajoled Israel. "Don't make us wait for the news."

Elspeth took the pipe from her mouth and blew a long stream of blue smoke in the direction of the fire. She looked Israel straight in the eye, opened her mouth a crack, and put the pipe back in it.

Emmy was chuckling out loud by now and it was borne in on Israel that he had not a card in his hand. "Oh, Elspeth, don't you be so hard. Tell us what you've heard."

"You first, Israel Hands, and then we'll see."

"Alright, alright," he yielded. "What do you want to know?"

"You can start by telling me about this treasure the Squire's chasing. How much is it?"

"Why, as to that... I'd guess about a hundredweight of silver bits and pieces."

"A hundredweight of silver bits and pieces. Well that would come in nice and handy for me, I don't deny. But I think the Squire might be disappointed." Elspeth chewed the idea over. "Yes, that would come in nice and handy. And what else is there."

Israel said nothing but it was obvious her guess had struck home. "Don't be so provoking, boy," she warned him. "Speak up. What are you scared of? You don't think I'd be chasing after it myself, do you? So what else?"

"Well, there was some gold as well," mumbled Israel.

"Good, good," Elspeth was getting excited. "Several hundredweights of silver and about the same of gold."

"No, no," Israel rushed to correct her. "There was less gold." His voice trailed off as he realised how he had been out-manoeuvred.

"So. Several hundredweights of silver and a bit less of gold. What else?"

Israel sounded sullen now. "There was some jewels and stuff, but that's all, I swear. And now the Squire's the only one who knows just where it is."

"And he's set to go chasing after it. And where did it come from?"

"Flint took it. It's his share, kept over a few years. And we took it from the Spaniards, so it's clean. And we fought d----d hard for it, too."

"Ah. Pirate treasure," Elspeth cut through his prevarication. "And it belongs to whoever may find it. How did it come to be lost?"

"Flint died in Savannah. He had yellow jack and died, and Billy Bones ran off with the chart, the dumb ox. If he'd had the wit to hang together, we'd all be setting up as lords right now. Instead, he's dead too and we've a deal of work left to do if we're ever to get hold of that chart again. But we'll have it, even if we have to turn highwayman to get it."

"Well, thank you kindly, Israel Hands," said Elspeth. "It seems you've got a tongue in your head after all. And now it's my turn.

"The Squire's off next Monday to Bristol. He's taken all the inside seats on the coach as far as Exeter. He's taking half his people along with him. He's written to a party in Bristol already, telling him to look out a nice ship for the voyage, and he's hoping it will be waiting when he gets there."

So here were our orders to get back on the road at last. There might even be a chance to retrieve the chart. We sat thinking what we should do next.

"With a bit of luck," said Israel, "we could ride up to Bristol on the same coach. That would be the sweetest thing. And if the weather don't get too miserable, it will be a fine trip into the bargain."

"I'd better go and get our places now then," I said. "There won't be many left if the Squire's taken all the inside seats."

"Tomorrow," ordered Israel. "You won't get to Bude early enough today. Start out early tomorrow and come back here afterwards. I don't want the Squire changing his mind and us not knowing. We'll go down Sunday night to Bude and we shall be sitting on top laughing at him as we stop by his gate. I believe I may even give him a hand up with his case."

Israel jumped up and bowed to his victim. "Why certainly, Squire, no trouble at all. It can travel up here alongside o' me. And don't you give it a second thought; I shall take care of everything." He laughed. "Ah, it's good to be moving again and quit skulking in these woods. Not but they're very pleasant woods, ma'am," he added quickly to Emmy, "but they don't compare to the sea, and that's the truth!"

Nor to Bristol, I thought, remembering the little we had seen of it as we passed through last autumn. The door of The Spy-Glass beckoned, and the thought of some fiery cooking from Mrs. Silver unsettled me. When had I last slept in a decent bed? Discounting the damp little corner I had in Bideford, it must have been back in Exeter. In Worthy's. I started to tell Israel again about that hostelry.

The two cousins listened for a while then Elspeth, realising we had left them in spirit if not in body, called us back to our surroundings. "If you two will rest with your drinking and eating pies along with pretty girls, it's time Lizzie and me were off, or the men'll be complaining. Now, Dick, Lizzie has a present for you. She came by it from the parson's wife, freely given so it's not unlucky. And I believe you'll need it more than her."

"You will keep it, won't you?" entreated Lizzie, clutching something under her shawl. "Or I won't let you have it."

"Get on with it, girl," said Elspeth. "Surely he'll keep it. Give it to him."

But Lizzie waited for me to confirm it. "I'll keep it, I swear. What is it?"

Shyly she drew out a small book. "Here. It will bring you luck." It was a miniature bible. A finely printed one in soft black leather covers. Page after page of tiny text that would need a good light to read.

I have it in front of me now, all these years later. Perhaps you have seen it on my shelves. It is stained and worn. The fine print is too small for my eyes now. What did I think of it then? Very little, almost nothing. I expect I regretted my promise to keep it but I was superstitious then, and it would have been very unlucky to break any promise concerning a bible. Of course, it was very pleasant to think that anyone should feel I warranted a present, and I felt grateful to little Lizzie. But not impressed by the Bible, even though I did keep it with me as you see.

Next day early I walked off to Bude to secure our places on the coach. On Sunday we rolled up our tarpaulin, said our thanks and goodbyes to Emmy, and stepped out.

It was a fine windy morning when the coach pulled up at the gates of Squire Trelawney's manor. A trap waited for us, loaded with luggage, and a crowd of servants and relatives surrounded the Squire. For all the extra hands, it took a long time to get the luggage stowed, and sure enough, Israel and I sat with one of the Squire's chests between us. Not, however, the one that contained the chart. That was presumably in the small writing box he carried with him inside the coach.

When we reached Exeter two days later, we followed in the Squire's wake as he moved into The Sun. He and his party would need most of a coach, and the earliest he could be accommodated to Bristol would be at the end of the week. After conferring quickly, Israel decided to take a coach on the morrow. I would travel up after the Squire had safely left. Israel had been thinking ahead and decided that the less the Squire saw of us, the better. We might need to hide ourselves from him in the future.

Duty done, we went down the hill to Worthy's, looking for a pie and a welcome. It was indeed a nice homely feeling to be welcomed by Mr. Worthy, who enquired after Caspar and the old shipmate we had been looking for. Israel had agreed that I should say only that I had not found Billy. Any mention of his death, or even the Admiral Benbow, might bring unwelcome attention. It was, I admit, even nicer to be welcomed to the board by Jenny and it looked as if my stay would be a fine holiday.

That evening we were content to bask in the heat of the fire, replete with good food and close to sleep. So comfortable were we that Israel even volunteered some personal information, something that had not been heard from such a taciturn and closed-mouthed man. He was, it seemed, from the nearby port of Topsham, the eldest son of a farmer-fisherman.

"Why don't you go back, Israel? You can spare a couple of days."

"Oh, it wouldn't serve. It never does to go back to any place you liked." He drew on his pipe. "I ain't free with advice. Let a man make his own mistakes, that's what I say, but I'll tell you this. If you ever go back to a place you was happy in, look out for sadness. And if you weren't happy in the place, why, it's madness to go back anyways. There's plenty of other places."

"But what about your family? Your mother, she'd be happy to see you."

"Gone. Long ago. And my father too, if there's any fairness in the world. He was a useless old drunk, anyways. My brothers and I would've been a deal better off without him." Such memories seemed to irk him. "Besides, I had trouble with the local justice. He's about the only person would be glad to see me back. How about you, boy? Don't you go home?"

But where had I to go to? My orphanage in Hereford had not a single warm memory to it.

Israel left for Bristol next day, and I followed only after seeing the Squire's party safely onto the Friday coach. The Spy-Glass welcomed me, and I found there the better part of the old crew. Long John, not wanting to feed idle mouths, had set them all to work painting, a craft with which all sailors are familiar. We slung our hammocks in the loft of The Spy-Glass. Mrs. Silver cooked, and we earned every mouthful of our rations by painting the tavern from tip to toe.

That done, we started on one of the quayside warehouses. Was it one of Long John's properties? It might have been, but I expect he persuaded one of his business acquaintances into having the job done, for a fee. He must have pocketed the money himself, for we saw none of it. He was liberal with the food and grog however, if not with money.

We had not long started on the warehouse when news of the Squire's plans began to reach us. He had busied himself with details he did not really comprehend, and was making a good deal of noise about it. Scarcely a soul in Bristol did not know of the expedition and its object. Long John locked the doors of The Spy-Glass that Sunday and told us how we would go about getting first the chart, and then the treasure itself.

"I call it right neighbourly of the Squire," he told us. "Bringing the chart to Bristol for us. If I'd knowed he was to do that, it would have saved Caspar and Dick a deal of sitting out in all weathers. And as if that ain't enough, he's going to fit out a ship for us. Our Mr. Blandy has sold him the Hispaniola for not much more than twice what it was worth." Mr. Blandy was a well-known character in Bristol. Now that he is dead I can say that he was a notorious buyer and seller of old cordage, rotten hulls and surplus victuals. He had a name for selling old nags as hunters. Long John must, at some time, have put him under an obligation for he was always exceedingly civil when he came to The Spy-Glass. Or perhaps he recognised in Long John a man of violence.

Long John went on. "I've put the word out, melads, that it would be an unlucky thing for just any man to ship in her. So we'll sign on, one at a time. We'll make like no more than ordinary sailors, and not let on."

How Long John got into the Squire's good graces I do not know, but he did and was soon working hard on victualling the Hispaniola. He got rid of a couple of the hands that did not suit him, and acted as agent to recruit the rest. He signed on all of Flint's crew that had come to Bristol, and made up the numbers with a collection of rogues and hayseeds he felt he could handle.

He also found Bent Arrow for mate. Arrow was a cross-eyed, drunken, old sailor wholly unfitted for the mate's berth. Perhaps ten years before he had been a man to reckon with, but now rum had rotted him to the core. Long John fed him, gave him a clean shirt and also just enough rum to keep him upright. Mr. Arrow (as he was to be known on board) berthed in The Spy-Glass under the eye of its host.

Long John had less luck in the matter of the ship's master, Captain Smollett. I am afraid the selection of that hard and honest mariner owed little to any acuity on the part of the Squire. We heard the Squire had taken him to oblige a lady. She was trying to drive a wedge between the Captain and her daughter, who welcomed the attentions he had been paying her.

Long John did not tell us whether he would join us. We imagined he would travel as passenger. All of us worried when we heard he would ship as the cook. No man can upset the crew faster than a bad cook. In the event, we need not have troubled ourselves. Long John ran the galley as competently as anything else to which he turned his hand.

I remember very well the chance that deprived us of Black Dog. It was a sunny spring morning shortly before we were due to sail. We had gathered in the tap-room of The Spy-Glass, just about all of Flint's crew that were still living, and were talking of times and ships gone by. A sudden hush broke over the room, and looking round I saw a smartly dressed boy standing on the threshold. This was my first clear sight of Hawkins, and I wish I could say more of him. I have in my mind a picture of an ordinary boy with a letter in his hand, uncertain of his welcome.

We did not know who he was, and would have hardly noticed him had he been dressed as was normal for boys in those streets. However, Hawkins, in his fine, clean clothes, looked obviously out of place. We all turned to watch him wavering nervously on the threshold. He stepped back and looked up at the sign for reassurance before forcing himself forward.

He stepped in and asked in a low voice for Mr. Silver. Long John hopped up to him and said quickly (and loudly enough for us all to hear), "I see you have a letter from Squire Trelawney. I'd recognise that hand anywhere." He held out his hand for the letter but Hawkins, in hopeless confusion, took it to shake and said, "How do you do?"

Long John laughed and said, "Let me guess. You'd be the new cabin boy, Jim Hawkins, am I right?" and Hawkins smiled happily. "Come in and sit yourself down by me. I'll get Mrs. Silver to make you a wet." Jim climbed up onto a stool and waited for Long John to return.

"Well, well. The new cabin boy. Tell me, Jim, my lad. Was you ever at sea before?"

"Oh no, sir. Only fishing. But I will do what I'm told. I really want to go on the boat."

"Ship, Jim lad, you must call the Hispaniola ship, God bless her. Otherwise we shall think you a landsman, no more. The Hispaniola's a ship."

"I'm sorry, sir. I try to remember. The Doctor told me the same."

"Never you mind. You'll soon get into the way of it. So what do you know about this here voyage? What does Squire Trelawney want, stirring so far from home?" Jim was too young to conceal his confusion at the question. He had been told not to let out a word about the treasure and was at a loss as to how to answer. He had just started to reply when he caught sight of Black Dog trying to slip out of the door.

If Black Dog had had the commonsense to grow a beard, or buy a new hat, he could have sailed alongside Hawkins until his dying day without being connected with the visitor to the Admiral Benbow. But the act of sneaking out confirmed his identity, and the boy raised such a cry and commotion that we feared all was lost. Except for Long John. He put on as fine a bit of theatre as you might see in a London playhouse.

He quickly sent George and Ben to run after the fugitive, who had left without paying for his drink. He asked if anyone knew the man, of course without learning anything. He even called out Tom Morgan and gave him a dressing down for drinking in such low company. He even had the wit to find out that Black Dog and Pew were the only crew members that Hawkins could recognise, and Pew was in no position to trouble us.

Hawkins soon fell under the charm of Long John's talk, and shortly the pair of them disappeared down the quay deep in conversation. Long John had his free hand on Hawkins's shoulder, except when he was pointing out things of interest on the ships they passed. The boy, swept away by Long John's attentions to him, was looking up at his face as if fearing to miss a single word.

Next day we went aboard. Getting a ship ready for sea is like trying to complete the spring cleaning before breakfast. So many things are needed to supply the needs of the crew. Tuns of water, barrels of biscuit, salt pork, dried peas, stockfish, flour. The Squire was generous in his provisioning, laying out for unheard of luxuries for the crew such as barrels of apples and even two smoked pigs. He was more than generous with his own supplies and case after case of wine and spirits were carried aft to the cabin, together with crocks of butter and conserves, cheeses, smoked eels and sausages. We also shipped enough animals for a small farm.

Shortly afterwards, the Captain came on board and set us to moving the muskets, pistols, pikes and cutlasses aft to the cabin. Here they would be away from the crew's reach. We thought nothing of it. Any captain would want them under lock and key. It only showed that Captain Smollett was no man's fool and knew something of his trade.

Our final day in Bristol brought a mad rush to lay aboard the last of the stores and supplies. Looking rather like a farm, a wood yard and a circus squeezed into a tithe barn, we got underway at dawn and crabbed down the river to the Bristol Channel, still hurrying to stow below those items we could, and to secure on deck those we could not. For once that difficult stretch of water was kind to us and by evening we sailed free in open water. Next day we left Hartland Point and the Admiral Benbow far behind. The Cornish rocks passed astern and we were alone in the Atlantic.

Smollett turned out to be a good hard master, who knew his place and kept the crew in theirs. No true sailor will be happy for long under a soft or incompetent captain. It matters not if the man shouts and swears at them, or rouses them out of their hammocks at all hours and works them hard. Always providing he knows his trade, they will be happy and respectful. Smollett knew that and dressed himself accordingly. He stood like a rock on the poop and looked every inch the king of his little sea-girt kingdom.

Bent Arrow, Mr. Arrow as we had to remind ourselves to call him, was more of a problem. He berthed with Smollett, and was liking his position less and less. Long John kept him supplied with grog, and listened in the privacy of the galley to long whispered complaints. Arrow was not a man to count on, and he was knocked on the head one night and dropped over the lee rail by Long John and Israel Hands. They told us next day how he had been set to go to the Captain and reveal everything.

Long John's plan was that Israel Hands should be the next mate, but the Captain's choice fell first on Job Anderson. Now Job was as slow as an ox when it came to thinking, and before Long John could explain to him again, he had accepted and we had a new mate. Not that Smollett took him aft to berth. Perhaps that was the reason for picking a man of Job's class.

The men who had not sailed with Flint were Long John's next problem. They had to be won round to our side before we landed. Flint's men had been split between the two watches and soon drew the others together into a crew. Nothing was said of our true purpose, as turning a man's mind to mutiny is not simple. That was left to Long John and Israel. In the meantime, the daily round of work and watching gave us the feeling of living in a family again.

The regular duties of the trade wind passage gave us many hours of cleaning, polishing and painting when I could watch our passengers. There is nothing like a sea voyage for getting to know the character of your fellow man. They can hide their true nature on land, but the sea will find them out. Hawkins, the Squire and Livesey spent much of the day on deck. Trelawney was little suited to the life of a mariner for he always wanted to be up and doing and the confinement of the ship obviously galled him. He strutted about the deck, poking his red nose into this and that. He was the image of a turkey cock, all fire and feathers.

The Doctor was a different case, small and sharp with black eyes. He had an inquisitive mind, and set himself to master the science of navigation. Once a day in the fore-noon watch, he would retire with Hawkins to the cabin to be instructed by the Captain. Sharp at mid-day, the Captain would shoot the sun, and the other two would stand beside him, sharing a sextant and attempting to duplicate his reading. They became quite proficient at it by the end of the voyage.

The Squire would have none of such things. His delight was to shoot, at sea-birds with a shot-gun or, when they had all been frightened away, with his duelling pistols at empty bottles floating in our wake. He seemed to have a large supply of empty bottles.

For me, the voyage was contentment enough. Sailing away from Old England meant that day by day the weather yielded and became warmer. Flying fish skipped from our bow-wave and the sun only clouded over to give us generous showers of refreshing rain.

But all good times must come to an end, and a curious fret grew up amongst the crew to be up and after the treasure. By the time we had made sufficient westing to be in the Indies, the image of Flints' stolen treasure had come to occupy a great part of our thoughts and private conversation. We mentally stroked the bars of gold and hefted them. We held the jewels up to the sun and saw it flash from their depths. I do not recall what I thought to do with the wealth. The treasure seemed to have become sufficient in itself. My friends underwent the same change, and it would not be exaggerating greatly to say the simpler men had become mad with it. I had the fever as badly as any of them.

Treasure Island

I am sure you are asking yourself if your old father is not making up a tale especially for you. You may believe how difficult it is for me after all these years to think myself back into the young man I was then. No one looking at my cassock could imagine a reformed pirate within.

Pirates are loathsome creatures and their ugly trade can have no excuse, not even with the blessing of His Majesty. As boy and youth I sailed with vicious men who had been steeped in the blackest evil. They thought of piracy as lightly as Mr. Hodges thinks of shoeing my mare.

You should not believe much of what you hear about pirates. People prefer to believe false and exaggerated stories of wicked deeds rather than the plain truth that, as always, is far duller. And the plain truth is that pirates are more like pick-pockets, or perhaps highwaymen, than the murderous villains of legend. I will tell you how we used to cruise with Flint.

He liked to cruise the islands of the West Indies because they always have a ready supply of water, fish and coconuts. We could put into isolated islands and stay as long as we wished. Few men o' war cared to come close into the islands, afraid of the currents and the numerous coral reefs which could sink them even in the gentlest of weather. We kept in touch with the island trading schooners that always had a bottle of rum or a parcel of fish for us. They also passed on information about ships expected to arrive or due to sail soon. They carried nothing and no one of interest to a pirate, but were nonetheless careful to behave with respect.

The ships we looked to intercept were the homeward bound vessels, carrying sugar and tobacco, indigo and spices. They always had money on board, especially when they carried passengers returning home to England after making their fortunes. We had only to meet one of these to be made rich men very quickly.

Finding a ship at sea is a difficult thing, much more difficult than a landsman might imagine. If you wanted to turn highwayman and rob the London mail coach, you would know where to meet it. You would merely hide yourself along the road and wait for it to come to you. But suppose the coach was free to travel not only by the London road, but might shape its course via Gloucester or Exeter. Then you might wait as long as you wished and never see a wheel of it.

A ship at sea needs no road and may travel wherever wind and weather allow. Your grandfather once described our task to me as being like a mouse searching for sixpence in a cornfield. In the end, however, a ship must come to port and this is where we could gather news of them. When we heard of one due to sail, we would wait just over the horizon and hope to outwit the Captain.

All ships at sea are wary of each other and will never allow a stranger to approach. Once a merchant captain realises he is being purposefully pursued, he has little choice but to submit. Pirates use light, fast vessels that mount real cannon. Their prey are heavy-laden and slow, and many merchants cannot stomach the thought of laying out good money for cannon and shot. They also hate the thought of shipping all that dead weight back and forth across the ocean along with the hands needed to fight the guns.

A merchant captain might try to run a little for appearances' sake, but in the end the exercise of comparing in the balance the value of his life with the value of the owners' cargo will induce him to heave to.

Pirates are practiced at rushing aboard a submissive vessel and securing anything they want from it. Neither crew nor passengers are spared, and anything of value is thrown back onto the deck of the pirate ship. While we were aboard our prey, I always found our victims behaved with great courtesy, trying to satisfy our demands and hasten our departure. Of course, they were terrified for their lives, and the sight of our cutlasses and pistols was usually enough to cow them completely.

We might set the sailors to dragging out any choice piece of cargo such as fine cloths or muskets, and we would relieve them of victuals and stores. Then, after cutting halyards and tiller ropes to disable our victim, we would be off. They were free to sail on their way, and we had supplied our ship for a few weeks and had a deck-load of booty to be shared out.

It is strange that most of our recruits came from the vessels we had attacked. There were always one or two of the wilder sailors prepared to volunteer if we needed them.

So why do pirates have such a bloody reputation? It is true that their absolute power over the people they seize leads some men to acts of insane bullying. However, for the most part there is no time to interfere with the passengers. And pirates are not likely to attack a vessel that is prepared to put up a stiff fight. If a merchant has a few guns and a fighting spirit, pirates will avoid the obvious danger and look for easier prey.

Pirates will fight if caught by a man o' war. They dread naval vessels for they know that a naval captain has at his disposal large numbers of guns and men. The Royal Navy also has a powerful avarice for the chests of treasure that pirates are popularly supposed to carry. (Need I say the truth is that every penny that reaches the crew's pockets is spent as soon as they reach port?) A true naval captain will not rest until a pirate vessel is stopped and her crew either dead or prisoners. Most pirates prefer to die fighting rather than be taken and hanged.

Another time a pirate vessel might fight is when he meets a like vessel. Some sort of perverse pride sets them against each other, scarcely needing the excuse of booty. These fights are rarely long or severe. In the last resort another pirate can always be bought off after inflicting a little damage.

So that is how pirates live. It is not a happy life, nor do most men follow it for long. They either fall victim to one of the debilitating diseases of the Indies, or they take up the office of crossing and re-crossing the Atlantic as an ordinary seaman. A few will be carried off by fighting, either at sea or more commonly in the grog-shops ashore. Even fewer will be marooned like Ben Gunn.

By now you will understand that pirates are not rich. They have no more chests of doubloons under their cots than you do. Most of them are too feckless to guard their money. They may be dead tomorrow or imprisoned (which amounts to the same thing after a short wait), and so they spend what they have without thought. They throw away their silver to inn-keepers, to loose women, and even to any little boys smart enough to dive for it in the harbour. That is a favourite pastime in tropical places. The boys swim out to moored ships and beg for money to be thrown to them. They are wonderfully at home in the water, almost like fish, and they think it no hardship to dive deep after the sparkling coins as they sink, come back to cry for more and again more.

Some men might save or even send money home, but the only one I knew who could claim to have a chest of treasure was Flint himself. We believed he kept it in his cabin for he would never allow one of us inside, not even for cleaning or the bringing of food. And after the taking of the Spanish galleon, the richest prize anyone had heard of, he had several chests in there. I believe the amount of the treasure weighed on his mind. Perhaps he realised that word would eventually travel up and down the islands, and one of his shore-bound friends might find it their patriotic duty to assist in his capture, if they were promised a share. So he decided to bury it on the Island.

I had landed on the Island twice before. Once for several days while we hauled down and careened the ship, and once just for water. On the occasion of Flint's visit to bury his treasure I did not go ashore, luckily as I later found out. We all knew something was afoot for Flint was steering somewhere definite, not just cruising around, but he would not tell us where. He brought us to the Island by night, presumably to make completely sure that none of us knew exactly where it lay. After breakfast, he called for a boat to be launched.

The weight of the treasure was tremendous. He had us bring from his cabin about a dozen small chests, all roped, tarred and sealed. Each one was a handful for two men, so I can guess that close to a ton of treasure lay hidden in those little boxes. We used a gin-pole to swing them out to the boat. Along with food, Flint had us bring up about twenty small kegs of rum, or at least, rum kegs. For in spite of their appearance they sounded to contain coins and not liquor. I later saw him taking silver coins from a similar keg, so I assumed that was what we heard sliding within the kegs as we swung them down.

Of course, Flint had a problem knowing who to take with him to the Island. He could hardly bury such a large pile himself, but taking a large party of men would put the secret of his treasure at grave risk. He took three men; William Allardyce, Kelly the Irishman and his cabin servant Snowball. Snowball was an escaped Negro slave, devoted to Flint, who acted as his valet, his butler and when trouble came near, as his guardian angel (if such an evil man could have one). He was a big powerful man, but a little simple and quite unable to speak due to a defect in his palate. He was the only creature Flint came close to trusting.

Before going over the side, Flint gave the Walrus to Long John, telling him to sail to the west where the Island could be seen from the masthead alone and to stay, putting back and forth for a week. On the seventh day he should return for Flint.

As the shore party pulled away for the last time Long John had us busy getting under way. We had already picked up the wind as the boat reached the shore. I was at the wheel and Long John standing quietly at the rail. I remarked to him that I would have liked to have gone ashore with them.

"No, you would not," he said emphatically. "At least we're not condemned men." I looked at him in surprise. "You don't think you'll see William and Kelly again, do you?" he asked. "You don't know Flint if you believe that." I did know him well enough to ask nothing more.

A long time later, after most of this tale had passed and gone, I spoke with Long John again about that trip of Flint's. I will try and recall his words as closely as I can for someone ought to record what happened, just to remember the lost souls of William, Kelly and Snowball. Long John and I were sitting alone outside his house. The rest of the household had gone to the beach to catch fish, and we were drinking rum and lime juice while we watched the sun set. I asked him, and this is what he said.

"Well, Flint wasn't a great one for talk, not with the crew, not even with me and me nearly a right arm to him. But one day we was sitting over a glass of grog, much like you and me now, and I asked him straight how come Snowball never came back. I was letting out I knew the others were done for, no matter what the weather. He fell to cursing William and Kelly, saying he had picked on them because they were not too clever, but they had turned on him. His plan went like this, you see. All four of them was to bury the treasure, then Snowball and him was to kill the other two and throw them in after it. That way the digging would look like no more than a grave, if anyone should ever try digging it up. That'd be the real Flint way of doing things. He didn't have no respect for no one, and using a corpse to cover his marks would come natural-like.

"But it didn't work like that, for William and Kelly must have got what little brains they had working side by side, and figured out what Flint meant to do. So they decided to let Snowball and Flint be while there was digging to do, and then kill the pair of them. So for a while they all worked together, all hiding their plans but Snowball, who didn't know nothing of what was to come. Flint said it was mighty hard work too, hauling all those chests ashore. By the time they were safely stowed, William and Kelly must have got worried that Flint'd have the jump on them, and they went to act before the kegs of silver were carried up.

"Flint said they picked a time when Snowball had gone for water. They went after him and the idea was that Kelly would attack him from the front, and William would stick him from behind. With Snowball dead the two of them should be able to handle Flint. But it all went wrong for them because Snowball was so terrible strong. You remember him, no holding him down. He latched onto Kelly, and William knifed him just like they'd planned. But when Snowball, who hadn't been fighting Kelly serious-like, felt the knife go in, he must have understood what was happening.

"He started to roar something terrible, and he just broke Kelly's neck. With his bare hands, like Kelly was a chicken. Didn't matter that William had the knife in him two or three times by now, he just kept shouting. He must have managed a swipe at William, and touched him too, for Flint said he was groggy and staggering about.

"When Flint ran up, hanger in hand, Snowball was still standing. Seeing his master, he took a couple of steps, reached out his arms, and fell right on him. William can't have been too bad for he took his chance to go for Flint, him having his arms full with Snowball. William reached over Snowball's back trying to poke out Flint's eye, but just gave him a nasty cut on the side of his head.

"Only he'd forgotten Flint's hanger, and Flint was able to stick him in the belly, as he'd come up from that side, you see. Old Flint had a black heart—you know that—and he sat telling me of William's face as he dropped his knife and clapped his hands to the hole in his belly. It turned me sick, if you want the truth. Then William ran off, still trying to hold his guts in. Snowball was dead by now, and Flint took his shirt to bind the wound on his head. I believe he pined a bit for old Snowball. They say there's no man so bad that a dog won't love him. Well, Flint had Snowball and with him gone, no one else would love him."

That is what Long John told me afterwards. All we sailors saw when we went back to the Island was Flint rowing out to us alone. He had swathed his head in a bandage stained with blood, and his face was white. He looked weak and feverish. None of us dared ask for the others, not then or afterwards. We were too afraid of the man.

Compared with some of the Hispaniola's crew, I was already an old hand at the pirate's life. I felt I had been born a pirate, and we had a dozen or more of Flint's old crew aboard. Aft there were the Squire's men, that is, the Squire himself, Doctor Livesey, Captain Smollett, Hunter, Joyce and Redruth (the Squire's servants) and, of course, young Hawkins. Then there were the other crew members, an assorted lot signed on by Long John and the Squire. Long John was working on these men to turn them into pirates.

"Turn they must," he told us. "They're either for us, or against us. And if they're against us, they can try sailing along without this barky under them." By the time we made our landfall there were only a few men undecided.

The Treasure Island looked a fine place the morning we sailed up to it. Dense green forest came right to the water's edge, hanging over in places and casting a dark reflection on the sea. In some places the trees grew back behind beaches of startling whiteness, so white that the reflected sun could hurt your eyes.

Many of the trees were coconut palms, the most useful tree I know. They are the strangest plant in appearance, but their distinctive shape and their rustling in the breeze are as much a part of the Islands as oak, ash and hazel are part of England. They do not resemble any oak or ash at all. Rather they are tall, rough stalks, thin enough that you touch your hands by reaching round them. The crown is an untidy clump of fronds, green and fresh in the centre but old and brown around the outside. At the base of the fronds hang the nuts, many feet above your head.

A man can live with just a few coconut trees to support him. The nuts are wondrous things. They grow to the bigness of a man's head, or even more, but much of that is a coarse and fibrous husk. Left to themselves, the nuts fall when they are brown and dry. Prise off the husk and inside there is a round shell as hard as stone. Smash that open and you will find a layer of moist, white flesh a half inch thick. Its flavour is rich and sweet. In texture it is perhaps more fibrous than most nuts. It certainly requires a deal more chewing than most. One mature nut like this will give a full meal to two men, and sufficient exercise of the jaw to satisfy a lawyer.

And that is not all. If your nut is gathered green and the top sliced off carefully, you will find it full of a refreshing drink, once tasted never forgotten. Bounteous Nature at her best has provided from a single tree both meat and drink. I can think of no finer luncheon than to sit in the shade by those clear blue seas and enjoy a fresh coconut. A slightly developed nut gives both drink and a thin immature flesh that can be scraped off using a chip of the husk as a spoon. How I long for such a lunch in an English January!

Gathering the nuts is not easy. Natives of those parts, whose toes are not accustomed to shoes, can manage by cutting steps into the trunks. Or else they manufacture rope by cutting a length of green vine and crushing the body of it with blows of the back of their giant knives. This primitive rope they tie into a loop about a foot and a half long. With this loop around their two feet, they grasp the sides of the trunk. Up they go, first hands and then feet, hands and feet, hands and feet, up thirty feet or more into the air. At the top they climb into the crown and down come nuts of all degrees of ripeness. Sailor though I was and accustomed to masts and rigging, I hated to climb the palm trees. By far the most frightening part was reaching back down out of the crown to start the descent, and I often wished I could stay up there forever rather than risk that first step.

Should you ever have the good fortune to see a coconut tree, let me give you a warning. Never, ever sit in its shade. The nuts can fall at any time and are fully heavy enough to put an end to you. It is a common fate for indolent young men of the Indies to be cut short by a coconut.

As we crept in to anchor, everybody was on deck and fretting to be ashore. No matter that we had been so long on board that a few more minutes could be no hardship, we all wanted to be off. I do not know if I thought to spend my time gathering morsels of Flint's treasure scattered freely around the Island, or if I just wanted to feel the warm sand between my toes. I had no plans beyond the desires of the moment, and I am sure that was the case for most of the others. How the next days were to change us all!

No sooner was the ship riding at anchor than we had two boats in the water full of men ready for a holiday on shore. Long John whispered to Israel, and he volunteered to stay on board with a small party. So wiser heads than mine were thinking of the future, but what did I care? We were off to find coconuts and barbecue fresh fish. Hawkins was the only member of the cabin party in the boats.

It must have been about this time that the horrible truth revealed itself to the Captain. Most of his men not only knew about the treasure, but they meant to have it for themselves. And being but a small party in the cabin, there was very little he could do to protect himself. Perhaps he thought of over-powering Israel and his men. If that could be done, there were men enough with the Doctor and the Squire's servants to sail the ship after a fashion. Perhaps it was fear or the thought of leaving Hawkins behind that stayed his hand. Anyway, I am sure a very worried band of men was left sitting in the cabin.

No sooner had we run the boats up onto the beach than young Hawkins jumped up and ran into the jungle. He would not answer to our call. But no matter, we had more interesting business to attend. First of all, coconuts. Myself and a couple of the younger crew members struggled and fought our way upwards and precipitated a thunderstorm of nuts on our mates below. Then, fully refreshed with coconut grog (made by mixing rum with the contents of young nuts), we took the boats and started out after fish. In water as clear as crystal glass, we floated over flower-beds of coral, with strange and wonderful colours in both plants and fish.

Corals take the place of the stone you see in our sea-shore pools, and by looking over the side of a boat, you can see many strange forms. You have seen them in Bristol curio shops, white rounded rocks made up of patterns of crystal blades. These sad specimens tell you as little about the beauty of a coral reef as a dried autumn leaf will tell you about the summer glory of a beech wood. Dull white is the least of the colours of a reef. There are red plants, blue frills of sea anemones, fierce black balls of spikes known as urchins, and many strange fishes wandering in and out of this colourful forest. Some might have the shape of a herring but all the colours of the rainbow. Others are taller than they are long, and have lacy fins and tails. Sea shells are not much seen around the reef, but they are there, as a short walk on the strand will show you. The natives of the Islands collect the living shells and clean them for sale. These are the glowing specimens people in England treasure on their mantel shelves.

Being so busy living their own lives, the fishes have less fear of men than you might expect. They are easy to spear and we were soon back on the shore with fish grilling over a fire. It seemed someone had carried with them a small keg of rum from Long John's store and stowed it in one of the boats. So in addition to the two bottles Long John had thought to bring, there was enough to make the whole crew roaring drunk, especially when taken under that fierce tropical sun.

For the most part, we were sprawled in the shade with the smoke of the fire keeping away the many biting insects. The crickets sang loudly in the trees behind us, and a sea breeze tempered the heat of the day. We lunched on fish and passed rum from hand to hand in coconut bowls. It felt very fine, and I remember thinking that the Island might be a very fine place to live my life.

It is a strange part of man's making that he will incessantly strive for a condition of happiness, but his conceptions of what is required for happiness are uncertain. A little girl might invest all her desires in a pretty ribbon from a peddler. A farmer might imagine that buying just one more field would make him happy. And having received the things they prayed for, are they happy? What fools we are, that we would reject the things around us the vain hope of happiness from something new.

So it was with us, surrounded by beauty and comfort in a form of an earthly Paradise, that we must draw the Devil out to lead us in a bitter and bloody dance around the Island.

The Devil Steps Out

As so often, it was rum that blew on the smouldering embers of discontent in the crew and brought them to a fierce blaze. While we passed the coconut shells from hand to hand our conversation became brighter and louder, and more incoherent. At least one man had reached a state of torpid insensibility, and I too was feeling very vague, when a shout demanded all our attention.

Tom Buckle, one of the Walrus crew, dashed the contents of his cup into his neighbour's face and sprang to his feet with an oath. He was a stocky man of, I suppose, some thirty years, clad in only a pair of sail-cloth breeches and with a red kerchief about his neck. His blond hair had already grown sparse, but what there was waved up over his crown in the breeze. His face shone cherry red from rum and anger as he stood swaying on the sand.

Long John was quick to call a halt. "Belay that, Tom!" he shouted. "What be you a-thinking of?"

Tom burst out indignantly. "That baby-robbing gypsy is telling me what I should be doing. Him, who's never been west of Bristol, letting on how we should be on board cutting throats and leaving you behind." He followed this with a wicked series of oaths defaming the man and wishing him back in the jail from which he had apparently just come.

The man (who I recall as Alan) was tall and dark, and from his curly black hair and cast of features, he may have had some gypsy blood in him. He was one of the new men. Whatever the root of the quarrel, Tom's insults touched something within him, and he hurled himself from the sand and crashed into Tom. We all leapt forward to pull them apart but we were too late. Tom had slumped to the sand with his life's blood pouring from a knife wound below his heart. We watched in horror as his face whitened and the life slipped quietly and quickly from his body.

Then beside me I felt a sudden convulsion from Alan as his head was pulled sharply back by the hair, and I saw Long John's brown right arm draw a knife across his throat, cutting deep and swift. Alan fell forward over Tom's body, choking horribly. None of us moved to help him.

Long John, having dropped his crutch, supported himself on my shoulder. He was shaking with anger, and I could feel the force of his emotion through the iron grip of his hand

"Poisonous gaol rats!" he burst out. "You're always the same when you get grog in you! Why do you think I brought just the two bottles? And who was it had to ship a keg? Was it you, Job Anderson? Don't think I haven't seen you whispering. 'Twas you put the idea in his head, George Merry. As long as I'm your captain, we'll do as I say. Let the Squire find the treasure for us, and he can't do that with his throat cut."

Job started to stutter under the attack, as he always did when he was excited. "I-I-I-I-I'm b-b-bo'sun," he got out. "A-a-a-an' you're c-c-c-cook!"

George Merry was ready to back him up. "You'll not be captain much longer, John Silver. You've made a mess of it with your high and mighty ideas, and now there's a good man dead. And it'll be the rest of us if you let that Smollett have his way. Do you think he hasn't got you marked? As like as not he'll put a bullet in you just when you step back on board.

"Job's right. You get back to your pots, and we'll go and take the cabin party."

"Y-y-yes," stuttered Job. "K-k-k-kill the s-s-s-squire!"

George started off again. "Job's the man for me," he said. "He'll sort out those lubbers. You've slipped your cable, John Silver. You've gone soft in the head. We need a real man to lead this crew."

Long John was furious. "Soft in the head, am I? Need a real man, do you? And Job's the one?" Some of the men nodded in agreement.

"So what are you going to do, Captain Job?" Long John sneered. "Kill all of them rich folks? Break out the wine and brandy, is it?"

"Y-y-y-yes, kill 'em," Job struggled to get out.

"And then what? Go for the treasure?" Job nodded, and Long John waved his arm at the forest behind "Where, you dumb lummox? Do you think Flint left it where you'd fall over it? You could be here for centuries and still not find it. And then what, Captain Job? Are you going to navigate the old barky home? You that can't even count your fingers?"

Long John rounded on George. "George Merry, you've a deal to answer for, filling poor Job's head with stupid notions. I know what your game is. You'll have Job make himself captain over my body, and then you'll be helping him aside. Well, it ain't going to work, George, because Job's not half clever enough to see me off. And do you think this crew is so ignorant they would be led by you?"

This stung George. "I'm as good a man as you, John Silver, any long day!"

"As good a man as me, you say. Well now, George Merry, since you've been making such a noise, you step up to the mark and tell us all what you want to do, then we'll have an election all nice and fair like."

George Merry made an unimpressive figure. Not well-favoured, his pock-marked face had a rodent look about it. He was short and stood slightly hunched. He was much given to letting the world know how he would do things differently if he had charge of the crew. Perhaps the amount of rum he had drunk stopped him seeing the trap Long John had laid for him. A sea-lawyer like George would never hold the respect of the crew against their old quartermaster.

"First off, we go for the Squire. Then once we've got the map, we'll ship the treasure and be off to Port O'Spain or somewhere." George defended himself, looking round to see the effect his stand was having on the men.

Long John sighed. "I see. And I suppose you'll be the first man rushing into the cabin? Or are you just going to knock on the door and ask for the chart? You'll have to get it sharpish, you know, or they'll just pitch it over the side and then where will we be? I'll tell you. After you've lost a deal of good men trying to break the cabin, we'd be left with nothing! That chart'll be gone, and without it you won't get a smell of the treasure.

"Don't you see? They can't lay a finger on Flint's gold without a bunch of us standing alongside them. So let them do the finding, and then we'll jump them, if you must.

"Now come on, lads. Tell George here how much you love him, and we'll be getting back on board like a lot of good sailor-boys. I suppose we'll have to let on that Tom is lost in the forest, along with this piece of offal." He poked at Alan's body with his crutch. "D--- his gypsy heart. I liked old Tom. Now pull them out of sight and we'll— By thunder, what's that?"

The echoes of a cannon shot rolled around us.

The beach to which we had come was out of sight of the ship, no doubt from Long John's desire to be out of the way of the Captain's long spy-glass. The shot could only have come from the ship and without a second thought all of us began to run along the beach towards it. Within a hundred yards the sand and the rum had begun to slow us down. Only Long John was thoughtful enough to travel by boat, his crutch being next to useless in the sand. The rest of us struggled through the bushes at the water's edge, then along another beach to a sandy point where we could see the Hispaniola.

The shot had come from the ship, and we could see Israel and the anchor watch readying the gun for another. We looked around for their target and saw, some way off, the Captain and a small party wading ashore with muskets held over their heads. We watched as they disappeared into the trees behind the beach. By common consent we started to run again,

77

seeking to attack the Captain. We had given no thought to our defenceless state but pushed on through the bushes regardless. Our foolishness met with the results you would expect. There was a volley of shots, and the leaders of our group came crashing back in panic. They had left behind one of the new hands shot dead but had, so they said, killed one of the servants with a rock.

"There's a house there," said George. "A little house with a thatched roof and a garden and all. Someone lives there." he added with surprise. At a loss, we took this piece of information back to the beach.

"Well, they've smoked us out." Long John appeared little put-out by the events. "That makes it more difficult. Now you boys be off and get the other gig. I'm going to see Israel and find out what's been happening. Then we'll make camp right here where I can see what's what."

I was one of the pensive group that made our way down to where poor Tom and Alan lay guarding the gig. We left them where they were beside the burnt out barbecue. Already the hand of Satan lay heavy on our island paradise.

We had lost three men that afternoon and soon found that Israel's party had lost another, shot by the Squire. It was a very subdued bunch that sat on the sandy point and listened to Long John. "Well, lads, we've thrown away a chance. If you'd listened to Long John we'd be walking out after the treasure this very afternoon, you may lay to it. But that's a tide we've missed.

"We'll set ourselves down here, keep a weather eye out for the Captain, and in the morning I shall go and have a word with him. He must be feeling a deal unhappier than us, for he's got no ship. I shall see what sort of horse-trader he is."

The Captain had discovered the cottage in the forest, and there his party had gone to ground. (You will remember this cottage from Dr. Livesey's book. It had been built by Ben Gunn, the pirate Flint had marooned there.) He had abandoned the ship to us, and perhaps he hoped we would sail on and leave his party in peace. And so we intended—once we had found the treasure.

We sought to forget our dead comrades with the plentiful food and drink we now had from the ship. It may seem strange but our spirits were high and we ran riot with no thought for the morrow.

The sun had already topped the coconut palms when Long John was about, stirring us with the end of his crutch. "Up, you drunken swabs," he was calling. "Up and see what real English gentlemen will do if you let them."

Realising something was wrong we followed him to where Salvation Luxton had crawled off into the bushes the night before to sleep off the excess of rum he had taken. Poor Salvation; he had come on to Bristol after selling some horses at Priddy Fair, thinking to have a quick look at the big world before returning to his father's farm. He had signed on after falling in love with the ships he saw. Now his Devon fields would not be seeing him again. As he lay sleeping someone had dropped a huge rock on his head, crushing it like an egg.

It was a sickening sight and my stomach rebelled. Breakfast was a sombre affair of cold meat and biscuit. As we ate, Long John gave his orders.

"First thing, I want to get Salvation underground. And Tom Buckle and the gypsy. Make sure you say some words over them. Then get back here and get yourself a musket and a cutlass each from the ship. Make it quick, for I fancy we shall be using them before long. You'll have to dive for them for they've been dropped out of the cabin window. Make sure you clean those muskets well. I don't want none of you hurting yourself." He stirred the embers of the fire with his crutch. "Dick, melad, you'll take me aboard. I've a mind to borrow the Captain's coat before I go and meet him in his country mansion." We all started to move, glad to have something to do after the debauch of the previous night and the bloody start to the morning.

In spite of the small piece of board he had pinned to the end of his crutch, it was a struggle for Long John to move around in so much sand. I could see his relief when he reached the hard packed earth of the path we took to Ben Gunn's cottage. It looked a pretty little place. Ben had built himself a small hut after the native fashion, with walls woven from reeds and a steep roof thatched with palm fronds. A deep shaded verandah ran the length of the front wall. All around grew clean, short grass parted only by a spring that ran from a dip near the cottage. A species of bush with hanging red flowers grew on either side of the doorway, and at random on the grass. In one corner of the yard Ben had planted a vegetable garden growing yams, tapioca and pineapples. To keep out the island pigs and goats, he had built a stout fence of split poles tied with creeper.

At the door of the cottage sat Captain Smollett, and it was he who answered Long John's call for a parley. I was obliged to wait outside the fence and watch as Long John attempted to barter the lives of the Captain and his supporters for the treasure. Smollett showed himself to be a remarkably hard man and yielded not an inch. Voices were raised and Long John stumped down the path exchanging recriminations as he came.

"They'll not play, Dick melad," he said as he came through the gate. "That captain's a blind fool. But we can wait. We've got food, and we've got the ship."

We walked back to the beach, and rowed to the point where the others were waiting. They were bearing and wearing the weapons they had recovered from the sea bed. Each had a cutlass and a musket. They had an assortment of knives, powder horns and pistols, and even two boarding pikes.

"Now, lads," said Long John, "We've a job to do."

"Aye, let's go and skewer them," said George, slashing the air with his cutlass. "I've a score to settle with Smollett."

"Belay that, George," said Long John sharply. "There'll be no skewering of no one. Leastways, not yet. Lie up in the trees round the cottage, and see if you can plug someone. Who's the best shot? Caspar, I believe that'd be you. Put a ball into that cottage maybe four times an hour. After a day of that, if they ain't dead, I'll see if Smollett speaks so high and mighty."

He looked to the rest of us. "Now don't you go blasting away your powder. It ain't going to last forever. Shoot at what you see, no more. Caspar'll do the scaring."

"What'll you be doing, Long John?" we asked.

"There's no use me coming with my timber leg and all. I'm going to set myself down here and maybe make some stew. Two men can come and get it after nightfall. Oh, and stay awake after dark. We don't want no more broken heads. Now, get on with you."

"That's all slop, Long John, and you know it." George Merry was furious. "We ain't going to lie up nowhere. These flies'll sting us mad. And there's only a few with the Captain. I don't fear them, if you do."

Long John sprang forward and, picking up George by his shirt front with one hand, held his knife under George's nose with the other. "I've had enough of you, George Merry. One more squeak out of you, and you won't have a gizzard to whistle through. D--- you, won't you keep your mouth shut for once? You'll lie up in those trees from now to Christmas if I tell you so. Now get out of here!" Long John threw him to the ground.

George was insanely angry. He started to get to his feet, "Why you—"

With a whistling crack Long John's crutch struck him on the knee. George screamed and rolled over, clutching his leg in pain. "George, you're stupid. Get him up and away, the rest of you. And I don't want to hear no wild shooting."

Long John turned his back and went to the fire. We trailed down the beach, taking the limping George with us.

The Assault

As we drew near to the cottage, we left the path and attempted to make our way silently through the forest. Off the path, the trees supported a tangle of creeping plants with thorns like brambles, and we needed a good deal of time and persistence to force a way through. A short detour like that is difficult at any time. For our party, with the necessity for silence pressing on us, it was a nightmare. I do not suppose we travelled this way for more than a furlong but it seemed much more. We ducked under low branches, pirouetted out of the grip of trailing vines, and clambered over the rotten trunks of fallen giants. In time, the forest darkness to our left eased a little as we came alongside the cottage and its garden. We were breathing heavily from the effort of moving silently through such a maze, and our nerves and ears were straining. At this point Israel nearly brought the expedition to an end by starting a wild pig from its sleep. Woken in confusion, the frightened animal ran back along the line of us, searching for an opportunity to break for the depths of the forest. You may imagine how our hearts leapt in terror as its low dark shape crashed past us.

It was impossible to believe we had not been heard but as we stood as still as statues listening to the noise of the pig running away from us, we heard not a sound from the cottage. Our rigidity slowly relaxed as nothing but the unending whine of the multitude of insects filled our ears.

Israel waved us to our places. I had to continue my journey to the far side of the garden and, once there, crawled forward until I could see the cottage through the leaves. The world lay at rest, with not even the insects disturbing the peaceful, sunlit garden in front of me.

Still no sound and no movement came from the cottage, and the heaviness of the air threatened to send me to sleep. The biting gnats that sometimes plague the beaches were absent, and nothing moved in the forest. I waited for the first of Caspar's shots at our enemies.

It came from somewhere to my left with all the suddenness of a thunder clap, and it must have passed through the cottage for I heard a cry of surprise and the sound of a pan falling. Then silence again. I settled down to wait for the next shot, reflecting on just how terrible the same wait must be within the cottage. I am sure the occupants were lying on the floor in the hope of safety.

Butterflies of many colours played up and down, in and out of the shadows and sun light shafts at the forest's edge. One of them, coloured a brilliant blue and fawn and much larger than our English beauties, was opening and closing its wings on a fence post in front of me. It was a time of unspeakable stillness. The butterfly rose, and then returned to its post to continue sunning itself. I thought to myself how strange it was, amongst all this richness of plant and insect life, there were no blackbirds or thrushes to sing sweetly.

After what seemed a very long time, Caspar gave another shot into the cottage. This time the smoke rose from the undergrowth on the far side of the garden. I waited again for the next shot.

When it came, it brought a hail of balls in its wake.

There was an immediate reply from the cottage, then several more shots from the forest on my left. As I watched, a party of our men led by Job Anderson broke cover and, crashing from the undergrowth, started to climb the garden fence. They were red-faced from effort and shouting crude war-cries to make their assault seem more terrifying. As they came up to the fence they threw their cutlasses over and scrambled up after them. Job was first across, with George behind him. The others quickly joined them. O'Brien slipped as he clambered over and fell back into the long grass.

I was surprised into wooden immobility as I watched them storm screaming across the garden to the back wall of the cottage. Here they were caught in a quandary for shout as they might, the woven walls were fully strong enough to resist a brutish onslaught. George laid hold of the barrel of a musket that had been poked through the cottage wall, and wrestled pointlessly with an unseen opponent for possession of the piece. All our men were shouting insensate oaths and meaningless cries, until the voice of Israel overbore them and called them to the front of the cottage where they might hope to affect an entry.

My attention went to O'Brien, a short man, who was still struggling to get himself and his cutlass over the fence. I heard myself shouting to him to throw the cutlass over first. He did not hear me. How could he from so far, across such insanity? He eventually seized on a thick branch to heave himself up, only to find it was dry. He fell heavily back into the grass again as it broke.

The cottage itself was a hornet's nest. The defenders gave volley after volley, obviously having more than one musket each but heedlessly Israel and his men ran in and out of the thick cloud of smoke that now obscured everything. The firing stopped abruptly and only the sound of blows and running footsteps could be heard. Men shouted and strained behind the fog, steel rang on steel and I could hear heavy panting. From the far side of the cottage, there came the noise of a scrambled rush. Then the

Captain's voice called to his men and all was quiet.

Slowly, the smoke drifted away to show two bodies lying on the grass. Both ours. Job Anderson had been cut down at the end of the cottage and lay sprawled in a pool of blood. I was shaking and confused. My musket was still loaded. It seemed there had been no time to use it.

My first thought was to get to the others, and I crept back through the forest, calling in a low voice. Israel and O'Brien were kneeling by Johnny. He had received a grazing wound on the head from a musket ball and lay conscious but helpless while he was bound up.

"Long John will string us up for this," muttered Israel. "That's seven men dead, yesterday and today, and Johnny here fixing to join them. More than seven!" He continued with the bandaging.

"What will we do?" asked O'Brien, never a man to follow his own path.

"I dunno, and that's the truth," said Israel, "But first you and I'll carry this one to Long John. Dick, go and find the others and lie low. Tell Caspar to keep popping shots over like Long John said. If he's alive. If not, do it yourself. There's muskets over there." He gestured to a large tree trunk.

As I went for the muskets, they picked up the groaning Johnny and started off with him. They took his arms about their shoulders and, weak though he was, his legs made some show of helping. It would be a long hard trip back, and only Long John's anger at the end of it.

The others started to appear from the forest, white of face and uncertain. They were as shaken as I, and immediately went on to help Israel and O'Brien. After such a disaster, they could not bear to be separated from their friends. I can well understand how a regiment of fine soldiers can fall to pieces in defeat. We all felt as weak and spineless as jellyfish.

Lacking any other ideas but reluctant to return to Long John, Caspar and I took two muskets each and crept from place to place around to cottage, Caspar firing through the woven walls. There were no shots in reply so the Captain, whose voice we agreed we had heard at the end of the fight, still had his men under control. It crossed our mind that there might now be more of the cabin party than of us.

As the sun started to set biting insects came out in abundance. In every tree there were large crickets harping, making an unceasing and maddening tumult. We could see flickers of firelight from the cottage, but heard no voices. We used the fire to aim our shots by but apparently hit no one.

In the end, the darkness of that unfriendly forest, the night noises and hunger eventually drove us to creep back down to the beach. Fumbling down the dark tunnel the path had now become, we saw first the grey luminescence of the sea and then gladly stepped onto the soft sand of the beach. A fire was burning at the point and beckoned us in. Sure enough, there were our friends with fish cooking over the embers, passing around rum punch. What a contrast their lively faces made with the hang-dog bunch that had crept away earlier on. Now the battle was safely distant, the good food and companionship made its memory milder.

In spite of our foreboding, Long John seemed pleased to see us. "Sit down, sit down, melads," he cried. "Here, move your carcasses and make way for two gentlemen as know how to do their duty. D'ye get any of them?" He listened as we told of our shooting, and questioned us closely about the action itself. "D--- fool, Israel Hands," he grumbled. "As good as murdered those men, he did. Smollett did himself proud seeing them off. But you didn't see the Squire or any of them fall, no?" He seemed to be taking the bad news calmly.

The storm of Long John's wrath had blown itself out again. Israel had been sent off with O'Brien to the Hispaniola on anchor watch as punishment, and Long John himself cared for the rest of the crew. True to his vast character, he had put yet another set-back behind him and was concentrating on preparing his flock of wayward helpers to try again on the morrow.

He let us talk on, passing the punch around, taking his grilled fish and biscuit until we had all relaxed and forgotten the difficulties of our position. Then he put Chips Morgan to watch, garnered the rum bottles and warned us for an early start.

We were woken in the blackness of a tropical night, a time soft and smooth, warm and almost friendly. Our plan was much the same as the previous day, except this time Long John would come with us.

The path up from the beach to the cottage was as black as a bat's wing, and we worked our way up holding the belt or shoulder of the man in front. I own that I had little stomach for what we were about to do. We had been light-hearted enough the day before, but now the thought of that cottage made my mouth dry and my inside tremble.

The cottage appeared as no more than a dark shape in the starlight when we arrived. Long John had us sit down quietly and ordered Caspar to put a shot through it to wake the occupants. He continued to shoot at intervals, moving from tree to tree. The rest of us lay still and waited for the dawn.

As the light came Long John hid us more securely and passed out biscuit to breakfast on. Then, when there was enough light to see by, we all started to fire our pieces at the cottage. The effect of a slow but incessant fire must have been crushing for the Captain and his men.

After about a quarter of an hour, when our muskets were too hot to handle and we were all begrimed with powder, Long John passed the word to cease fire. He hailed the cottage.

"Ahoy there! Anyone still living in there?"

"We're living, Silver," replied a voice. "And we'll live long enough to see you hang for this."

"Oh, my gamecocks! Still got fire in you? Well, you'll have to catch me before you can swing me, and that's not so easy, wooden leg and all. Enough of that. I want another talk with the Captain under a flag of truce, that's why I'm a-calling you."

At first, there was no reply, presumably the occupants were consulting, and then the voice came again, "Step up then, Silver, but no one else."

Long John passed the word again. "Don't nobody shoot, nor move nor anything, or I'm a dead man." He fought his way through the undergrowth to the path and swung up to the gate. Working hard, he made his way up to the cottage past the bodies of our comrades and stopped outside. The Doctor came to the door to parley.

There was no altercation this time, but a long and complicated negotiation. The Doctor would speak a little with Long John, and then step back out of sight. Then out again for more discussion, and back again, and out again. Both started to gesture to the back of the garden, and towards the beach until, at last, Long John offered his hand. The Doctor hesitated and then shook it. With a smile on his face, Long John started back down the path.

"Come round here, lads," he shouted. "Caspar too. Stand you just outside the gate. Point that thing at the sky, Tom Morgan, you lubber. Uncock it. In fact, uncock everything. I don't want no stray shots now."

We gathered at the gate pointing our uncocked muskets at the sky. Long John had obviously struck a good bargain. "It'll go like this, boys. I'm going back up there and the Doctor, bless his soul, is going to give me the chart." He waved our questions aside. "Later, later. Them and I are going to walk over to the back end of the garden and they're going to leave over the fence. Once they've got clear, you can come in. Just stand there like a line of bollards until I give the word. They'll have a pistol on me, and they're shy. You do any more than just stand there, and they'll plug me for sure." He went back up to the cottage.

So Long John finally had his way. As the inmates of the cottage filed out we found we were looking at a small group of strangers.

The Doctor and the Squire were smaller, beaten. The Captain had been wounded and was helped along by Gray. And Long John looked taller and finer. Well he might, for he had at last got his hands on what we had been searching for—the chart, freely given to him by the Doctor as they passed through the fence. He called us over and we rushed up to the cottage. Inside it was dirty and strewn with scraps of straw and firewood. A metal pot with a shot hole in it had been up-ended in the centre, as if it had been used as a table. The supplies which had been carried from the ship were stacked along the wall. At one end lay a body with a bloody kerchief over its face. One of the Squire's servants.

I do not think any of us noticed that Jim Hawkins had not been with the Captain's party.

"We've done it, boys," Long John exalted. "See what happens when you listen to your old captain? And if them dead men such as Job outside had more than ballast in their heads, they'd still be here along o' us."

We were all crowding round for a look at the chart but Long John was afraid of getting it torn in the rush. "Belay that," he said. "I shall keep it. Now, Caspar, cut along to the ship and warn Israel and O'Brien to keep a weather eye on the shore. I doubt the Captain'll try to get aboard, but he might. And then come back here. Dick, run up to the point and get two shovels. We've folk that want burying all over. And Caspar'll help you bring Johnny here where we can tend him." As we left, Long John was getting Chips, Morgan and George to clear up the cottage.

Indeed, there were not many of us left, but we were enough to sail the ship to Port O'Spain, and there was always the consideration that the less that sit down to supper, the larger the shares of pie will be. So we had a happy trip, jogging down the earth path, winding along under the dark jungle. Through the arched trees I saw the sea, of a calmness and blueness that you never see in England. The white line of coral sand grew to either side and the ragged heads of the coconut palms were still for once. As we broke out onto the strand we realised immediately that something was wrong. The ship was missing.

Scan the horizon as we might, it was nowhere in sight. What could Israel have done? The two of them could hardly have sailed it away. We hurried up to the point that we might see farther. It was no good. The sea was empty and unfriendly. Loading up with shovels and some provisions, we turned back. With Johnny hanging from our shoulders, the way seemed harder and longer now.

Back at the cottage, Long John seemed little put-out. "Israel will have had his reasons," was all he would say. "He's moved the ship out of harm's way, that's all."

That night the positions were reversed. We held the chart and slept in the cottage. The Captain's party was sleeping under the stars.

Hawkins Comes to Visit

It was a restless night for all of us, made worse by Johnny groaning and whimpering as he drifted in and out of sleep. Long John brought it to an abrupt end by hammering four bells on a pan outside the cottage and shouting to us to stir ourselves.

"Rouse yourselves, you lubbers," he shouted in to us. "If it wasn't for old John here, you'd all be murdered in your beds. A tidy line of little Salvation Luxtons, God rest him." Long John had been on watch to keep us safe, and also to give himself time to think.

"I needs to know what's afoot," he told us with the air of a decision made. "I needs to know what the Captain's up to. But first we'll have breakfast, an' I'll have some of that coffee the Captain was kind enough to leave. So get brewing. I ain't cook no more, specially for you lot of wasters, though I've poked the fire up for you."

We shook the sleep out of our limbs and went to the cooking fire, set in a clay oven to the side of the cottage door. Soon the smells of hot coffee and hot beans woke our insides too, and we sat to eat and listen to what Long John had to say.

"First off," he said, "We've got the chart. A good thing too. An' I know it's real for I've seen it before. A bit less marked, but it's the same chart Flint made. Second off, the Captain's got it too, for I know he made a copy. He'd be crazy not to.

"That don't signify. They'll not be able to touch the treasure without we know about it. And we'll not be able to touch it without they know about it. Again, that don't signify for there's more of us than there are of them, especially counting Israel and O'Brien. And the big thing that we have and they don't, is the ship. They're counting on us taking the treasure and leaving them a few nails and such-like so they can make a launch and sail along after us. They don't want to see no treasure now. They just want to see next year.

"But I don't trust 'em. No, not one inch do I trust 'em. That Doctor especially, gentleman that he is, he wouldn't think nothing of plugging one of us, if he could."

Long John was sitting on some firewood with his back to the cottage wall, poking with his crutch in the dust in front of him. "Well now, the first thing we must do is to find Israel. And I ain't fit to go running about this blighted tangle. Dick and Caspar had better do it for us. I believe we'd better get ourselves back inside where no one with a musket can see us. You two get up to the top of the island and see if you can find the ship.

Then come back down here and tell me what's what."

"Oh, John," whined George. "We don't want to sit here all day. Let's go after the treasure."

Long John looked at him hard. "George, you've a deal too much lip. The treasure will be there tomorrow, or even next month if that's how I want it. We've got the ship to worry about, and the Squire with those great long pistols I'm sure he had stuffed inside his coat." We looked apprehensively at the forest that loomed all about us.

"Get moving, you two. Take a musket and a pistol each, and a cutlass. They would dearly love to put an end to any of us if they could. It would even up the odds. Get back as soon as you can."

While the others moved inside, we kitted ourselves up and walked rapidly to the fence. We aimed to climb straight up the hill. Whoever had lived in the cottage (it was Ben Gunn in fact) had obviously been a tidy man, for the undergrowth had been cut back two or three yards from the fence. As we clambered over, we faced a tangled green wall of creepers, giant grass and thorn bushes. We were obliged to cut our way in with our cutlasses. Beyond this wall, in the shadow of the forest, it was a little easier to move. The trees being so great, and their branches so interwoven, it was dark and quiet within. There is an atmosphere of heavy silence in such a place, a heaviness that can smother a gunshot a hundred yards away. Any hope of navigating through such a maze must rely on a compass. In winding your way around the great tree trunks and clumps of undergrowth you can soon become hopelessly lost.

We had only to head up hill, however, but we had a care to blaze a trail for our return. We pushed upwards, perspiring freely and plagued by flying insects trying to settle on our faces. Abruptly the upward slope stopped and we found ourselves on a narrow ridge running obliquely across our path.

Here the forest trees yielded enough to admit fingers of sunlight, to let us get our bearings, but not enough for us to see where we were heading. Forced to choose one way or other along the ridge, we chose the wrong one and after a while found ourselves dropping down. Reversing our steps led us to a subsidiary summit, still veiled in trees. By now we were beginning to learn a little of the maze in which we found ourselves and succeeded in selecting the right way to follow, leading to another hillside. A short climb later and trees started to fail, and we found ourselves obliged to struggle through chest-high grass, grass whose blades were so sharply edged that our forearms were soon etched with shallow cuts which stung in the heat. The higher we mounted, the lower the grass became until we stepped out onto an area that had obviously been recently burnt. New green shoots were sprouting from the blackened earth and promised to blanket it again in a month or two.

Behind us we could look out over the forest to the sea beyond. The dense black-green of the forest swept down to the sea, flat and smeared with the marks of tides. In places the forest and the sea were separated by beaches of brilliant white sand. Off-shore of the beaches lay coral reefs, and the quiet lagoons between reef and strand showed every hue of turquoise above the sandy brown of the coral. But search as we might, the Hispaniola was nowhere to be seen.

At the summit of the hill, two wild fig trees stood in the thin grass, and we found signs that someone had been there before us. Stones had been arranged at the foot of the trees so that a man could sit comfortably with his back to their trunks. Here in the shade we drew our breath and peered out across the sea. Who else had used this lookout? Who had sat here long enough to polish the trunks of the trees against which we lent? Who had dined off the coconuts whose shells lay scattered in the grass?

The view of the other side of the island was similar, and similarly deserted. From our lookout we could see nearly all the shoreline. Just one sector at the southern end of the island was shielded by a low hill. We sat in silence, pondering on what could have happened to Israel. And then again we pondered on the phantom person who lived in the cottage and had spent many hours up here watching the horizon.

Idly scanning the shore, my eye was taken by a movement. A brown banner was waving over the tree-tops. We peered hard and the vagueness resolved itself into a scrap of sail, a fore-topsail maybe, for a bare main mast could be made out a little way aft. Even from that distance we could see the ship to which they belonged was heeled over, probably aground on the beach below the palms.

Here was news indeed! Our minds raced over what could have happened to Israel and O'Brien, and how the ship came to be grounded on that side of the island. Stranded where she lay, she would be a sitting duck if the Captain and his party came across her. No matter how she had come there, the course of our duty was clear. We must hurry down to the others so that Long John could set her rescue in hand.

As we left the hilltop we came across a path leading off in a westerly direction. In spite of the virtual certainty that the path had been made by the owner of the cottage, and that it would eventually swing north to reach it, we returned on the trail we had made and slid uncomfortably down to our friends. Here, to our surprise, we found the Doctor tending Johnny's head.

"There you are, boys," called out Long John as soon as he saw us. "D'ye get any pig?"

"Not exactly," replied Caspar following his prompt. "But we saw one a good way off." That would set Long John's mind at rest.

"So when will he be up and about again, would you say?" Long John asked at the Doctor's elbow as he bandaged Johnny's head again.

"If he is lucky, if he is very lucky, he may be suffering from no more than a headache two days from now." The Doctor finished off the bandage with a bow. "On the other hand, it may be a week or more. So feed him what he will eat and keep him away from bright lights and loud noises. They'll only make him suffer unnecessarily. And let us all hope that the fever does not get to him." The Doctor made as if to leave.

"Wait a bit, Doctor, wait a bit," cried Long John. "Will you not take a grog while you are here? If you're kind enough to visit Johnny, a little home comfort is the least we can offer."

"I'll take some of the Captain's coffee, if you please," said the Doctor a little stiffly and moved outside. We joined him there, believing his presence would protect us from stray musket balls.

"So how's Captain Smollett keeping?" asked Long John, fishing for hints of our enemy's strength.

"Well enough," said the Doctor. "Well enough to see us all home. And how are you proposing to navigate yourselves away from this island?"

"Oh, don't you worry about that, Doctor," chuckled Long John. "The lads and I know these waters like you know your parish. And I don't believe we are over anxious to sail to England. The Squire would have something to say to that. And how are you hoping to get home?"

The Doctor seemed just as confident as Long John. They planned to make themselves a boat of some sort and then sail from island to island hoping for an early rescue. He seemed to have accepted the loss of the treasure with equanimity, something that should have worried us if we had noted it.

After taking his coffee, the Doctor rose to leave. "I shall come back tomorrow, Silver. Listen for my call."

"Why thank'ee, Doctor. That's handsome of you. We shall have the coffee waiting, and may be some breakfast if you have time."

Long John saw the Doctor to the fence and came back eager for our news. It obviously troubled him. "Now what's Israel about? Drunk, I'll lay. He's probably wandering up and down the shore looking for us. Let's hope he doesn't chance on the Captain or we may have to wave him goodbye."

He thought a little longer. "We'll have an anchor watch tonight, lads. And beware of what you shoot at. It might just be Israel or O'Brien. Then tomorrow if they haven't shown their faces here, we shall have to go and look for 'em." And he started to make up the watch list, warning us again to keep an eye out for the others.

I drew an early watch, from eight to ten o'clock, always my favourite. Young people find it hard to stay awake late into the night, unless they are dancing, and I preferred to get my watch over early that I might go to bed tired and still have nearly a full night in which to sleep. I hated most watching between midnight and four o'clock when a person's spirits are naturally low. Work is always harder, cold is colder and the wind seems to blow sharper at that time.

I took my station in the vegetable garden behind the cottage. In spite of my friends being only a few steps away, I felt a dread of the surrounding forest and could not help remembering poor Salvation. Accordingly I sat down amongst the tomato plants where I would be concealed, and I listened very carefully.

The night was still but far from quiet. All around insects whirred and chirruped. Glow-worms blinked in the bushes and an occasional bat fluttered through the clearing. My two hours trickled slowly on.

It must have been near the time for my watch to end when I became aware of someone or something approaching the fence. Whoever it was obviously did not feel the need to conceal his approach as he climbed the fence and, coming into the garden where there was a little more light, I saw the figure was too slight to be either of our friends. Luckily his way passed within a few feet of where I was crouched. As he passed I dropped my musket and, leaping onto his back, over-bore him and pressed him to the ground.

My shouts brought a scramble from the cottage and when I loosed my catch we found we had caught. Jim Hawkins! "Why, Jim lad," cried Long John, as surprised as the rest of us, "Why, you've come to visit us. Are you planning to sign on as a pirate?"

Once we had led Hawkins into the cottage, he looked about him with an expression of dull incomprehension. "Where's the Doctor?" he blurted out. "You've killed them!"

"No more we have, bad luck to them," said Long John equably. "Are you hungry, Jim? Here, give the boy something to drink and poke up the fire. We must entertain our guest."

He set himself down against the wall. "Come along, Jim. Draw up a piece of floor and sit alongside old John here. Tell me what you've been up to. How's the Captain?"

"But where is he?" asked Jim, obviously completely confused at the turn of events. "He was here when I left."

"Ho! You went and left your friends here? Why did you do that?"

Jim looked sheepish. "I don't know," he mumbled with the normal excuse of a little boy caught doing something naughty.

"So what have you been doing? Picking coconuts?"

"I went to the ship. I went sailing."

In spite of his concern, Long John's face did not betray a thing. The rest of us stopped where we were and if anyone had had a pin to drop, it would have made a noise like an empty saucepan. "And how's my Israel?"

"He's dead." Jim looked at the floor, and then at the rest of us and suddenly his face crumpled and burying himself in Long John's jacket he started to sob. Long John wrapped an arm around him and, waving us to get back to preparing food for the lad, gave all his attention to Jim.

"There, there, boy. You tell old John about it. What happened? Was they fighting?"

"They got drunk," the boy gasped out between sobs. "They were drinking brandy. They kept sending me for more, and then they started fighting. I tried to stop them but Israel hit me away. Then he cut Paddy's throat and the blood went all over him." The horror of the moment renewed the boy's weeping and Long John could only keep caressing him and wait for the whole story to come out.

"And Israel?" asked Long John after the boy had quieted a little.

"Paddy had made a hole in his stomach. He went white and sort of sat in the scuppers. Then he fell over and died as well. I didn't know what to do. But the wind was behind so I steered for the beach."

"Well done, Jim lad. We'll make a sailor of you yet. Did you drop anchor?"

"I ran her on to the beach instead. I-I think she touched the reef as she came over. Then we hit the beach. I tried to drop the topsail, but I couldn't so I just let all the sheets go. I pushed them both out of the entry port into the water and they sank to the bottom. Then I swam ashore and went to sleep on the beach. Later I found a path and followed it to come here. I was tired." His voice tailed off as a plate of pork, peas and biscuit arrived.

"And some grog," Long John ordered. "He's had a hard voyage and done a good job." Jim ate hungrily, taking large swallows of his grog. He'd hardly finished eating when he started to fall asleep. In a daze, he allowed himself to be led to a corner and was soon sleeping deeply.

"Now here's a turn-up," mused Long John. "Israel choosing to soak himself in the barrel. Half-witted swab. Now he's counting fishes along with O'Brien, d--- him! So first thing, we'll cut along and make sure of the ship."

"But the Doctor's coming," someone said.

Long John thought a little. "You're right. We can't have him getting wind of where we're going. And I want him to see that we have Hawkins. It might make them a bit careful about shooting into the cottage. Then again, it might not, but we can only try. So, we'll wait until he's gone." With that we went to sleep.

Next morning we busied ourselves in expectation of the Doctor's visit. Johnny was a little brighter but still looked very pale and complained of a crushing feeling round his head. Long John turned his attention to Jim. "Now Jim, I don't know if you're here as a volunteer or if I should call you a pressed man. No matter; I want you safe and out of here when the Doctor comes. Now, Dick. Get yourself some line and splice an eye about his middle. Keep the other end tied to your belt or something. Jim, I shall want your word that you will not run, or I shall have to tie your hands and feet as well. What do you say? Speak up now. Say it nice and clear—I swear on the Bible not to run. Has anyone got a Bible?"

Of course there was a Bible, the one the gypsy girl had given me. That raised Long John's eyebrows but he said nothing. Little Jim took it in his hands and spoke the words. Then we settled back to wait for the Doctor. As soon as he arrived, I was to take Jim out into the garden, far enough that they could not speak to each other without shouting.

Long John was worried that Jim might give out the story of the ship. His concern was misplaced. As soon as the Doctor came, he told us some unwelcome news. The Captain's party had chanced upon the ship and secured her. Long John let him change Johnny's bandage, then showed him to the gate. Apart from a shouted greeting, the Doctor had no conversation with Hawkins.

Long John stood speaking with the Doctor for some time before he finally left. He spoke to us with a cold fury. "D--- Israel Hands and all his works. See what too much grog does? Not only does he get himself killed but he's nigh on killed us too. The Doctor's crowing over how they got the ship, and wishing us joy of the treasure.

"There's only one thing to do. We'll dig up the treasure, and then try to do a deal. Get them to set us ashore somewhere in return for a good cut of it. So, get moving!"

It was a small band that set out on the path to the beach to hunt for the treasure. Death had laid his hand heavily upon us, and he would continue to reap his grim harvest.

Where the Treasure Lies

The first part of our journey led down to the boats. We were, in truth, surprised to find them under the trees where we had left them. We assumed the Captain would have rowed them away but wherever his party had hidden, it was not near this beach. We took both of them with us reasoning that would be safer. And besides, we hoped to fill them both to the gunwales with gold pieces.

With our little expedition divided into two, we rowed slowly around the point. We had two or three miles to cover to reach the landing where Flint and his three companions had gone ashore, and short-handed as we were, we made a slow trip. The heat of the sun had dried the boats out more than a little, and Long John and the boy kept busy bailing and splashing water over the woodwork.

We ran the boats up onto the beach where a small creek ran out of the swampy forest. The trees grew dense and tangled on the flat ground to our left but hilly ground lay behind them and round to the end of the beach just over the creek. This is where Flint and his men had landed the treasure. The beach was unmarked, of course, but there still seemed to be an old trail running through the edge of the trees to the high ground. Perhaps the wild pigs kept it open, or perhaps someone else. Certainly it had not stayed like that since Flint's visit. The forest would have closed over it long ago.

With our hands full of tools, cutlasses, muskets, and water skins, we cheerfully abandoned the boats and pushed inland. There were but six of us and the boy. First of all walked George Merry and Caspar, with the chart. Then Jim, still tied to my belt. Long John puffed along behind me, and Chips Morgan was helping Johnny in the rear. Johnny had refused to be left behind alone no matter what pain it would cost him. He looked very pale and close to collapse.

Our first object was to gain the height of a grass-covered rib that ran inland, eventually climbing up to the lookout with the two fig trees at the summit of the island. From the rib we might be able to survey our path onwards. So through the sharp-edged giant grass we pushed upwards, cursing the heat, the insects (of which there were many) and our own clumsiness. At least we were blessed with some kind of a path, which made our progress much easier. On reaching the crest of the rib, we found the grass a little sparser and shorter. Here we stopped to get our breath and take our bearings.

The map was of little help now, and we followed the written directions around the edge of the chart. They directed us to a prominent tree about a mile south-south-west of our landing. This was to be our starting point. As we regained our breath we looked south over a waving expanse of green-brown grass. For some reason there were no trees on this hillside. It was as if less rain fell here than farther north, if two different climates could exist on such a small island. I say no trees but there were stunted trees and straggling palms in the small valleys that ran down to the sea. And also isolated stalwarts that somehow managed to scratch an existence amongst the grass. One of them stood south of us, not far away. Not an impressive tree, a twisted thorn-like bush no bigger than a cider apple. There were no others, so this must be the one for which we were looking.

Long John reached for the chart. "Let's see what we're about. East-by-north. That puts it over there somewhere. But we won't find it in this cover without we follow the directions. Dick, you stay here and help me keep hold of the boy. The rest of you get over to that tree there. Caspar, take this." He brought out from his coat a brass pocket compass larger than a watch. "Three hundred and seventy paces east-by-north from the tree. Now all of you count them out separately, because we have to find 'the pointer', whatever that may be. Do your three hundred and seventy paces, and stop where you are. Then I'll come up and we'll start searching."

As Long John settled himself down beside the path, the rest took to the grass. Off the path, movement was a struggle. It required considerable force to thrust through the waist-high tangle of grass. Slashing at it with a cutlass proved useless. No matter how sharp the cutlass, the force of a cut was spent on only a fraction of the stubborn grass. Dick Caspar returned for a shovel and found that a way could be forged by holding it horizontally across his body and using the handle to press the grass down step by step. A very slow and tiring way to break a path and we could see the three fit men taking turns at the work while Johnny followed in their wake.

Without shade and without the benefit of a breeze, the sun beat down harshly on us. Long John pulled his hat forward the better to shade his eyes, and I blessed the old straw hat I wore. He cleared his throat. "Dick, listen here. Now the others are away, I've got something to say to you by way of a warning."

His tone surprised me. Although he was always polite enough when addressing his men, he never confided in them. He kept the growth of his plans private, and we just concerned ourselves only with the orders that resulted. I was surprised, and shocked too, for his manner suddenly suggested a lack of confidence in our doings. His eye caught little Jim watching intently and he spoke to him directly. "Jim lad, clap your hands over your ears and don't hear a word of what I'm going to say. Not a word, mark you, or I shall have to put you where you won't tell no tales. Sit over there where I can see you." Jim promptly pressed his hands to his ears and he sat uncomfortably, looking like one of the wise monkeys.

Keeping a close eye on Jim, Long John began to unburden himself. "Dick, I don't know for sure, but I believe we're in deep trouble. That Doctor had a bit of a talk with me, and there's a couple of things. First he's got someone helping him. I don't know who but I'd guess it would be whoever built that cottage. Second, when we find the nest, I'll lay it's empty, for he didn't seem like he'd be missing anything. 'Watch out for squalls' is what he said, no more. Watch out for squalls.

"Now, Dick. Your friends there—our friends—they be good enough men, all of them, but they might turn vicious if we was to find an empty nest. There's no telling what they might do, and I shall need someone to watch my back. And then there's the Captain and his men. I don't like being here, for this is just where they might expect to find us. If you've got an enemy, don't go strolling in his garden, that's what I say. But we've as good as invited them along to take potshots at us." He looked searchingly around us, peering at the long grass and I thought how things would be if the Squire were to get a clear shot at us.

Long John went on. "Truth is, Dick, I've halfway done a deal with the Doctor. The boy's life for mine. If I make sure the boy's alive, they'll set me ashore somewhere safe. It ain't much of a return, to be sure, but it's a deal better than leaving my bones on this cursed island.

"Now I won't be doing that deal if I can help it. There's not much in it for me, and it's even poorer for you lot. But it may fall out that way, so watch out for it."

"What do you want me to do?" I asked, my head in a whirl.

"Just watch out, that's all. You take care of old John and I shall take care of you. If we get separated and we get out alive, go you to Port Domingo. Go to Bewley's, the chandler on the seafront—you'll soon find him— and ask for Mr. and Mrs. Gold. He'll set you right and you'll find old Sally if you don't find me. And if I do turn up my toes here, pass on my love." He looked away from me, obviously in the grip of emotions that a young bachelor could not understand. The signs of his human weakness hit me like a blow to the stomach. We sat in silence.

After a few minutes, Long John came back from his reverie. Jim still had his hands pressed to his ears but his face was showing distress at his uncomfortable position. John laughed and motioned for him to relax. "Well done, Jim. I likes to see a boy who does what he's ordered. You'll go a long way, if you live long enough to leave this island."

Looking over at the others, he stood in indignation. "Look at those lubbers! What's Chips about now?" Our friends had reached the tree and were now involved in the business of counting paces. Not an easy job, fighting their way through the grass, keeping on a bearing and counting all at once. Morgan had obviously lost count and gone back to start again. We started along the path to meet them as they emerged from the grass.

Johnny, Caspar and George came up slowly, pacing careful and faces closed from concentrating on their counts. George stopped a few yards from the path. Caspar came on and crossed it by a few yards. Johnny came to a halt near George, but Chips Morgan was thirty or forty yards short.

"You can't count," called Long John laughing richly. "Come over here. Dick, give me the boy and cut along and bring back the rest of the tools. Stay where you are, you three."

After marking the stopping places, we started to search in the long grass, looking for 'the pointer' mentioned on the chart. It was not long before George found it. "Bones," he called out. "There's bones here."

"Don't touch nothing," ordered Long John. "Let me have a look."

In the grass two long bones could be seen. "Don't touch nothing," repeated Long John, "Cut this grass back." We hacked at the grass with our cutlasses and soon a pattern of bones made itself clear. It was the skeleton of a man.

"Where's his arms? Clear away over there." Long John pointed above the eyeless skull. The skeleton was complete. A man lying on his back with his arms high above his head. The bones had been whitened by the sun and were dry and porous. Scraps of clothing lay about the bones and a dry cracked leather belt circled the segments of spine below the collapsed ribs.

Long John stirred the faded rags with his crutch. "Blue. What were they wearing? Do you remember? Snowball didn't have no shirt. Allardyce. Tom. He had a blue sailcloth guernsey. Am I right?"

We said nothing, thinking of the four figures rowing ashore in the heavily laden boat long ago. And of Tom Allardyce, whose last remains lay at our feet. And of Flint, rowing back with his bandaged head, alone.

"Where's his belt buckle?" asked George curiously. "He had a big buckle with a girl on it." He rooted in the grass. "No knife neither. Someone's been here, poking about."

Long John was more interested in the way the skeleton lay. "Why's he lying like that? It ain't natural. What was he about?" We considered the puzzle. Suddenly Long John pounded his hand on my shoulder and laughed. "The pointer! Flint's pointer. That poisonous buzzard used poor Tom as his pointer. So it's forty-four paces down there. He pointed down the sharp slope that fell away to the tree-covered swamp below. The way was pretty much in the same direction we had been following from the tree.

"We've got to bury poor Tom," said Chips Morgan. "It ain't right he should lie like that."

"Later, after the treasure," said George, already moving down the slope. We rushed on, forgetting to count our paces in our haste to reach the end of our long voyage. Fortunately, I remembered Long John's warning and held back a little.

The rush led down to the line where the giant grass gave way to the swamp forest. Here we found what Long John had feared, an empty nest. A pit had been dug out, perhaps six feet square and three deep. The yellow stony soil from the pit had been piled all around it, and some had fallen back in. Grass had started to grow through the edges of the spoil and no doubt would overwhelm it completely in a couple of years. A piece of broken board and dried leaves were all the pit contained.

Try and imagine our feelings at that moment. All our dreams of wealth lay destroyed. Our striving, suffering, travelling was all for naught. Our blood had been drained to no account. We were left with nothing.

At this critical moment, I was standing above the pit beside Long John. Johnny had gone to the edge of the pit, but the others had jumped down into it hoping that whoever had rifled the treasure might have overlooked something. Of course they found nothing.

Frustration turned to fury as George looked up at us. "You knew about this, Long John, you swab! You and that Doctor, I knew you was up to no good." Shaking with anger he whipped out his knife and started to climb from the pit. He hesitated as he found himself looking straight up at Long John's double-barrelled pistol only a few feet away.

"George, I've—" Long John's words were torn away by a volley of musket shots from the slope above. Johnny pitched head-first into the pit, knocking down Caspar and Chips. George seemed not to hear the muskets but when he saw Long John was distracted, he resumed his murderous climb out of the hole. Turning back, Long John fired one shot, catching George square in the forehead. He fell forward, half in and half out of the pit.

Long John clasped the boy to him, holding the pistol to his head, and shouted "Run, boys, run! Into the trees before they re-load." I hesitated but Long John thought faster. "Run, you fool. I'll be alright. God bless you, but run and I'll see you in Domingo. Go!"

Searching for the Silver

In our panic we thought nothing of the thorny tangle through which we crashed, seeking concealment from the Squire's long musket. Barbed vines tore at our flesh and clothes, toothed palm leaves raked our arms and faces. The darkness of the swamp swallowed us up.

Only three of us were left now, a minor remnant of the Walrus's crew. Caspar was there, old Chips Morgan panting harshly and looking very scared, and myself.

"What do we do now?" moaned Chips.

"The boats!" said Caspar. "Quick, before they get to them!"

We hurried on, trying to shape a course to the sea but passing only where the forest permitted. After only a short run we found ourselves standing in a dry water-course that crossed our path. Without consultation, and not withstanding that it would carry us to our right rather than straight towards the sea, we followed it deeper into the forest. We soon passed into the depths of the swamp and our pathway filled with water.

The water-course ended abruptly where it joined a sluggish brown stream. We plunged waist-deep into the warm water and started to follow the flow down towards the sea. The vegetation on the banks was an impenetrable tangle so we had little choice. The bottom was surprisingly firm considering the swampy nature of our surrounding, and the vicious vines did not obstruct our way. On we rushed, the water sometimes below our knees, sometimes up to our chests. The stream wound this way and that, but its ultimate outfall would be the sea. If we had had our wits and the leisure, we might have noted that our easy passage was no accident. The trees had been cut back, and fallen branches removed to the banks.

After an age of struggling we finally burst out of the darkness into the scalding sunlight of the seashore. The sea's mirror doubled the blaze of light up at our faces, half blinding us as we sought to get our bearings. For once fortune seemed to have shone on us. The stream by which we had left the swamp was the very one near which we had come ashore. And there were the boats, at our feet. With the last of our strength we heaved first one and then the other into the water. Caspar and I took the oars of the leading boat, Old Morgan being useless by now. He slumped in the stern gasping, and without comprehension of what was happening. He had picked up a nasty wound below his knee and was bleeding freely, but if there was any pain he had yet to feel it.

As we pulled, Caspar and I scanned the grassy ridge up which we had been walking such a short time before. We could see no sign of life, although we thought we were sure of the position. We had moved far enough already for the lone tree to come into view, and we imagined we could see the trampled grass about Tom Allardyce's last resting place. But no people, not until our eyes wandered upwards towards the lookout at the summit of the island.

Creeping slowly upwards across the grassy flank of the hill was a small procession. Instantly a feeling of safety swept over us, and we rested on our oars. We could make out five figures. The boy was the clearest as being smaller than the others, hurrying on ahead. And by his gait we could also make out Long John, who must have been labouring like Hercules to force himself up that hill. I said nothing to the others about Long John's arrangement with the Doctor.

"Where to now?" asked Caspar. "We can't hold the cottage, just the three of us."

"I don't suppose they'll be thinking of attacking us," I said. "They'll have other fish to fry. They've got to get the ship ready to sail."

"Have they got the gold?" Caspar wondered aloud, "If they have, they'll only hurry the more to get away with it. You're right. No matter what, they'll not be interested in coming across for us. What'd be their gain? I still don't fancy that cottage, though."

"Let's get there quick, before they can," I said. "Then we can take what we want and get back to the point where we started. We'll be safer there." There was not much shelter at our first camp, but at least we would have a clear sight of anyone coming. The air was also a good deal fresher out on the point, an important thing when you are in such fever-ridden country.

So it was. With Chips minding the boats, we hurried up to the cottage, coming back with two small biscuit barrels, some salt pork, a large bag of oats and a small but very welcome one of coffee. At least we should be able to survive for a while. We pulled the boats up at the point and while Chips made a fire, I climbed one of the coconut palms. Still keeping a weather-eye open, we made ourselves comfortable and rested from the cares and scares of the day.

We kept a watch that night, but saw nothing.

Next morning were surprised to see something on the beach at the point where the path to the cottage emerged from the trees. It looked like a small cairn of rocks with a white flag flying above it. Scarcely taking our eyes from this apparition, we slowly ate our breakfast. We tossed from one to the other ideas on what it might be, and why it should be there. I believed it might mark a message, possibly an invitation from the Captain to re-join the Hispaniola. He must be desperately short-handed and might have decided to be magnanimous.

Caspar was more inclined to suspect it as a trap and to guard ourselves we decided to approach by sea. As a double assurance, Chips and I dropped Caspar off on the beach some distance from the cairn. If it was a trap, the thought of Caspar and his musket behind the ambush might serve to protect us. He disappeared into the trees and we rowed slowly on.

We need not have feared. The top rock of the cairn held a down a letter for us. Written on the folded paper was the following:

To the Mutineers.

This is to assure you that, in spite of your mutiny and the hurts you have done us, we mean no evil to you provided you make no move to attack us. If you are prepared to help us, we will do the same for you.

Captain Smollett instructs me to make the following offers to you. Firstly, we have need of one of your boats. We are prepared to leave you supplies of food, sail-cloth, cordage and other necessaries in return for one boat. If you agree, leave the boat here by the cairn and return to your camp. We will immediately bring some supplies, and the rest will be left before our departure for England.

Secondly, while we have located Flint's gold we believe there is still a substantial quantity of silver yet to be found. Should you be fortunate enough to locate it, we are prepared to allow you to purchase a passage to a safe port without fear of prosecution as mutineers and pirates.

Do not forget that we will be watching you. Even as you read this we are watching. Any attempt to interfere with us or our business, or even to move north of this point, will be met with death.

Yours, in earnest,

Livesey

Taking the warning to heart, I looked up and down the beach, searching under the trees for evidence of the threat about which I had just read. There was nothing, nothing to be seen at least. I called Caspar out from the trees and he came trotting down to read it for himself. We agreed immediately to comply. As we waved Chips in, I noticed the neck of a bottle protruding from the cairn, a brandy bottle. A friendly gesture in deed.

The choice of boats was quickly made. Both were in good condition but the one we had left at the camp was some six feet longer. The size of a boat is very important if you plan to cross the open ocean, and the larger one would give us more protection and a better chance of arriving. We beached the smaller boat near the cairn and walked back to the point. Chips was suffering from his wounded leg and our progress was slow.

On reaching our camp we sat below the palms watching the boat drawn up on the beach some five furlongs away. Two figures emerged from the forest, both carrying bundles on their backs. They were heavily laden and plodded slowly up to the cairn. We could almost hear their sighs as they shrugged off their burdens, and started to heave the boat down to the sea. Minutes later, they were aboard and pulling north. If they were bound for the other side of the island, they would have a hard journey.

We wasted no time launching our own boat into the water and rushing to see what had been left for us. True to the spirit of the exchange we found food in plenty, an axe, some log line and a tarpaulin. There was also a short note saying future communication should be by letter left at the cairn. When there was a letter, the flag would be left flying.

As we pulled back with our booty, our minds naturally turned to winning our passage home. If it was true the silver had not been found, we should devote ourselves to finding it. It was our assurance of a safe passage home. The alternative would be a long and dangerous journey in an open boat. None of us was conversant with the mysteries of true navigation, something I now regretted bitterly.

Flint's chart with its written directions was still in Caspar's pocket. It was very clear as to the location of the gold, and we had found its old location quickly, in only a couple of unhurried hours. However, Flint seemed to have treated the silver almost as an afterthought. The only reference to it was a cryptic note 'Silver in a like place butt nearer too'. When we got back to our camp we spent some time peering at it and wondering what Flint had meant. We had much of the day left to us and we resolved to start our search immediately.

It was strange to start again up the path to the grassy ridge. Hope was returning to our young hearts and the memories of the day before did not weigh unduly upon Caspar and me. They may have weighed more heavily on old Morgan as he limped along behind us. The wound on his leg had grown red and swollen, and he walked in obvious pain.

Our first goal was the empty pit that had held the gold. The buzzing of flies and a terrible smell led us there. George and Johnny were still lying where they had fallen. Decay had already advanced horribly in that tropical climate. As our stomachs would not allow us to bury them honestly, we could only grab the scattered tools and hurry back up the slope. Our companions would have to wait for nature to have its way before we could return and lay them to rest.

Sitting a little way off, we pondered again on Flint's words 'Silver in a like place butt nearer too'. 'Nearer too' could only mean that the silver was concealed nearer to the tree which had served as a sign-post. But the description 'in a like place' was more difficult. The gold had lain at the swamp margin, where the flank of the ridge falling sharply had met the flat, forested swamp. Not an easy spot to reach if you had to carry large chest of gold along with you.

We moved first to the tree and spent the rest of the afternoon in forays down towards the sea, looking for a sharp bank that we could consider 'a like place'. Our search was fruitless. The little valleys running off the hill behind us were all round bottomed, and harboured only a few scrubby, dry palms with hanging leaves. There were no sharp banks with dense thickets at their foot. Added to that we soon moved too far from the tree and had continually to return to the tree and start again. Morgan's leg was troubling him badly and he spent the afternoon under the tree, leaving Caspar and I to struggle through the long grass looking for signs.

It was a heavy hearted trio that left the tools below the tree and headed for home. We had been unsuccessful on our first day, but we would be back.

Chips Morgan slept very poorly that night, and woke in a fever. He would only take a little water and was obviously not going to be able to help us for at least one day. His leg was badly swollen, marbled with red flames, and walking would have been impossible. Making sure he had everything he might need at hand, we left to continue our search.

At the end of an exhausting day spent combing the hillside above the tree, we returned tired and thirsty to find Morgan raving in the grip of a deep fever. His case was obviously much worse than we had thought, and his wound seemed to be poisoning his whole body. We resolved to leave a letter for the Doctor at first light. Morgan's cries and struggles kept us awake far into the night. Towards dawn his delirium seemed to lessen and as we fell asleep he was breathing hoarsely through his mouth.

Caspar woke me by shaking my shoulder. "Chips is gone," he said. Morgan lay as he had the night before but both of his eyes were staring up at the sky. Yet another of Flint's crew would not be leaving that hateful island. Before eating, we dragged and carried his spineless body some way down the beach and, turn by turn, began the weary business of making a grave. Shovelling sand over his staring face made us both sick at heart. From my Bible I read over him Psalm 107, the Mariner's Psalm, for he did go down to the sea in ships and make his business on great waters.

We were keen to leave our camp that morning, but less keen to return to our dispiriting search. Under the excuse that we needed fresh food we spent the day fishing and smoking our catch.

Next day our energy was renewed and we returned to the task, though with little hope of success. Accordingly, when we had gained the height of the grassy ridge above the landing place, it took little to persuade us to sit down and contemplate our surroundings.

When worrying over a puzzle, a man's mind may become over-full of calculating. New thoughts and inventions are swamped by a sea of contingencies and suppositions. A new mind coming fresh to the problem might cut through this enveloping web. Failing that, complete relaxation may allow a shaft of light to penetrate an over-loaded brain.

"How would it be," I mused carelessly and not really thinking about what I was saying, "if 'nearer to' didn't mean nearer to the tree? Perhaps it's nearer to something else, like the gold."

"Couldn't be the gold," Caspar seized the idea. "The silver is 'nearer to' than the gold. But nearer to what?"

"The beach? The silver is in a like place but nearer to the beach!" I was shouting in my excitement. "That's where Flint started out. It must have been hard enough getting the gold to where it was, so he buried the silver a bit nearer. Nearer to the beach."

We stood up and scanned the forest below. The abrupt change from swamp to grass followed the foot of the slope, winding crazily in and out as the sea of the forest lapped against the coast of the hills. Here indeed were plenty of 'like places', all the way back to the beach over a mile away. Dropping down to the trees we started to traverse the foot of the slope.

It was a tricky march. The slope was very steep and we found it difficult to maintain a footing. It required that we should have one leg markedly shorter than the other to maintain an even keel. We began to realise that the constant winding of our course added considerably to the distance.

We searched for any signs of a disturbance, any indication that the ground might have been dug up. And we found it! In a wide embayment whose floor sloped more gently into the trees was a longish mound, looking for all the world like the grave of a giant. It lay half hidden by grass and encroaching creepers. No force of nature could have made such a thing.

We hurried up the slope to the tree to recover our tools. Working feverishly we beat back the scrub and started on the lower end of the mound. The difficulty of digging in that oppressive heat soon slowed us down. We had continually to enlarge the hole to give ourselves room to dig, and to stop the spoil falling back into the hole. The soil was not compacted and came easy to our shovels. Progress was fast and the hole deepening rapidly when two things happened simultaneously.

Firstly, Caspar's shovel struck something that made a hollow thud, and at the same time he flung his shovel aside and leapt back with a frightened oath. Sticking out of the dirt at the bottom of the hole was a broken, rag-covered bone.

"It's a grave!" Caspar whispered in horror. We had been disturbing someone's last resting place. A moment later we were sitting halfway up the slope above, appalled at what we had done.

I felt unsettled in my opinions. We had definitely found a body, and not a native one, judging by the remnant of clothing. And the grave, if such it was, looked far, far too big. The mound must have been ten feet long by five broad. Flint had taken three companions with him on his expedition. We knew where one lay, a mute pointer. Had we discovered one of the others? It would be just like Flint to cover his treasure with a pair of corpses, just to put any finders off the trail. I determined to dig farther to find out what Caspar had struck. But I worked alone as Caspar would have nothing to do with opening a grave.

It was with some trepidation that I scooped away the soil and extracted the bone, which I lay carefully to one side along with some more fragments. And underneath, as I had suspected, lay the silver. The top of a keg had been broken open by Caspar's shovel and, amongst the dirt which had fallen in, shining coins could be seen.

Shaking with excitement, I squeezed a hand in through the hole and drew out three silver coins between my fingers. We were saved! Caspar, his niceness about disturbing bones forgotten, embraced me and throwing tools aside we climbed up the slope and raced to the beach. We had to write our news to the Doctor as quickly as possible.

We rowed straight to our camp but stopped only long enough to fetch paper for our triumphant letter. Only when we returned to the boat did we realise the view over the beach had changed. Floating at anchor just outside the reef lay the Hispaniola. The Captain had refloated her and our finding of the silver had come just in time, for he would surely not delay his departure long.

With light hearts we rowed on to the cairn and left word of our news under the top stone. We picked up the flag and set it fluttering its call in the late afternoon breeze. We returned to our camp to cook and to watch for our message to be picked up but to our disappointment there was no movement on the beach before nightfall.

We woke early next morning, rising with the sun to start what promised to be an exciting day, but our hearts leapt to our mouths when we saw that the Hispaniola had gone. Not a ripple disturbed the empty sea to the north of us. The flagstaff on the cairn was erect with its white flag hanging limply.

We wasted no time getting into the boat, not pausing even for breakfast. I expected the worst and the message we found justified my fears.

Our letter had been recovered and answered by another.

To the Mutineers.

We are about to embark for England and, as promised, we have left supplies on the beach about two miles north of here. You are well equipped and victualled, and with good fortune should be able to escape. The Captain tells me that you should steer to the north-north-west and expect a landfall after three or four days. If you then follow the coast to the west you will quickly come to Port Domingo. On our part we undertake to leave no news of you, good or bad. If your pasts find you out, it will be without our assistance.

God be with you,

Livesey

Under these cold words, in a more ragged style probably due to the darkness in which it was written, was another message.

I have just read your message concerning the silver. I regret that we have already considered taking you aboard, silver or no, and decided the risk was too great. I will, of course, represent your position to the Captain but I believe the fact of your find is unlikely to change his mind. We only put you to the task to keep you diverted and had no expectation of your success. I am sorry, but you have only your own dangerous natures to blame.

Livesey

We looked at the empty anchorage and knew then that the Captain had given his answer. The injustice of it all crushed us and I believe we were both close to weeping in our dejection.

Marooned

We were alone, marooned on a deserted island. Our friends had gone or lay dead. The Hispaniola too had left us. We were two young men surrounded by an empty and limitless sea, too shocked for the moment to order our thoughts.

It is hard to convey the awful loneliness of our situation to you who have never been far from the next human being. Think of it. All through your life a good shout would have come to the ears of another person. Can you think of a moment when that would not have been true? Now try and imagine how we felt, knowing that there was a real chance that, for as long as we lived, we would never see another mortal soul.

We sat beside the cairn and railed at the Captain, the ship, Long John, Providence itself that had cast us aside. But that was a dry and profitless occupation and soon we had mustered enough curiosity to go and seek the goods that had been left for us. We rowed up the coast.

The Captain had been generous. He had left cordage and sailcloth, biscuits and pork, carpenter's tools, nails and timber. We had a quantity of line and fish hooks of various sizes, so we might look for fresh food. Lying on top of the pile was another musket with its accoutrements, balls and powder. Shirts and trousers for three persons. A kettle and a skillet. Three mugs and a tinderbox. A small keg of rum and a leather bag of tobacco. We were at least handsomely victualled. There must have been enough there to support us for two months, and it would last much longer if we supplemented it with our own efforts.

As we loaded the supplies into our boat, our minds turned to the future. We must endeavour to escape from the island. We were both certain about that. Our boat was conceivably large enough for such an enterprise, and it seemed that Captain Smollett agreed with us. It would need some attention however. If we were not to row all the way to Port Domingo, we must have a sail—at least one, two would be better as we would be rigging our vessel fore and aft. And we must load it with sufficient food and water to last us for, say, a week. A boat that is to brave the wide ocean must be in the best of conditions and I could already see small items that would need attention. And while we were working on the boat, we would have to survive somehow. We could not expect to go on sleeping in the open. My thoughts raced over the problems, getting a mast stepped in our boat, building a shelter against heavy rain, providing water butts for our escape, digging a well to draw the water. And what about the silver? Would we take it with us or leave it where it lay, or should we move it to another more private spot? And George and Johnny still unburied? We had a long list of tasks still ahead of us.

However, the longest journey starts with a single step and in our case the first small step was moving our supplies to our camp. Then we determined to spend the rest of the day making ourselves more comfortable. A shelter was the first requirement. We set two stout saplings in the sand, with another tied between them, and draping our tarpaulin over it soon had the beginnings of a substantial tent. Then we devoted ourselves to a hearth built from coral rock taken from the beach. Palm fronds did service as a floor inside the tent and our little house began to look homely. The crew had spent several days living at the point and had left a deal of rubbish to mark their stay. After picking it up, we carefully cleaned the sand outside our tent and got our campsite ship-shape. By the time we had completed these preparations, the sun was falling rapidly to the horizon and the cooking fire took our attention.

We did not stint ourselves in the matter of food that night. Whatever the future might bring, tonight we needed comfort and took it in the form of a generous meal. Indeed, the fullness of our bellies did in some part alleviate the emptiness we felt in our hearts. As we lay on our backs, watching the tropical stars wheel above us down to the still mirror of the ocean, we made our plans. First of all we would get our boat into shape for a long voyage. Then we could at least set sail with some confidence that we would come safe to land. Then we would attend to George and Johnny. We both wanted our friends to be buried properly.

Finally, there was the silver. Here we had a difficulty, not only from its considerable weight but also from pirates. We knew (who better?) just how we would fare if we were caught at sea with such a treasure. And if we came to port, how could we land it in safety? It was impossible that we should row into the harbour of Port Domingo in a boat loaded to the gunwales with silver. Quite apart from the land-based thieves we might expect to meet, how would we answer the voice of authority with its inevitable questions? Such a quantity of silver is not normally to be found in the possession of two poor sailors. So we elected to carry what we could in our pockets and hide the rest. There would be no difficulty getting a lugger or something similar to retrieve it, once we had sailed to Port Domingo and found out how and where we could safely bring it ashore. Best of all, Long John could help us, if we could only get to Port Domingo.

Men at sea live for long periods with only their own resources to fall back on. As a consequence, they rapidly become adept at a strange assortment of trades. They can sew, they can make and mend shoes, barbering holds no mystery and carpentry little more. All of these are in addition to the more normal parts of seamanship, so the setting up of our boat to venture on an ocean voyage worried us little. We had the sailcloth and sufficient rope for rigging. It was simply a matter of time before we would get the boat ready. But rather than get on with what we understood, we decided to recover the silver first. It seemed more interesting.

Next day saw us carefully laying aside the mingled bones of Snowball and Kelly to get at the silver beneath. There were twenty-four kegs, all neatly bound in tarred canvas. Considering they had been buried for three years or more, the canvas was in remarkable condition. Only one keg was in any way damaged, the one we had hit on first. Setting the silver to one side, we reburied the bones of our old comrades. The grave lay as I have described it, at the foot of the grassy bank running down to the swamp. In case anyone should ever wish to find it, it is I would guess, about three furlongs from the beach, at a point where the ridge above draws away from the trees for a space. Our friends' bones were laid in a grave that seemed far too large for the dry white sticks that used to be living sailors on the Walrus. They had the best burial we could give them, and surely better than they had received from Flint. The rest of the day we spent shaping a head-board with our hatchet, so their last resting place was marked for a short while at least. Decay is so rapid in the tropics that the monument will surely have been worn away only a few years after we set it in the ground.

That night, sitting at our cooking fire, we felt the contentment that follows a good day's work. For the morrow we had only to move the silver and bury it again. Then we could set about preparing for our long voyage.

Carrying the silver to the beach would have been both long and arduous. The heavy kegs were worse than pigs to carry. Pigs at least have legs that you may grasp, even if they do wriggle. The kegs had nothing and their weight and roundness would soon force our grip apart and down they would go. We thought about constructing a stretcher so that we might carry them one at a time to the beach, but then we arrived at the idea of taking the boat up the stream into the swamp and carrying the kegs only the short distance to meet it. We found the way easier than we had expected. The gold must have been removed in the same fashion and the passage had been made simple by the clearing of fallen trees and hanging creepers. Nonetheless, man-handling the kegs down to the boat was hard labour and we did not reach the camp with our booty until late afternoon.

The next day we buried it in the forest behind the near the point, taking a bearing on one of the rocky headlands to the north of the beach. Experience had already taught us how quickly the vigorous trees and creepers could change the appearance of the forest and that was the reason for selecting a more permanent bearing point. How could we know just when we would return?

Fitting out the boat took us several days. First we pulled it up, cleaned it, and set about repairing and caulking it. We cut ourselves a stout mast green from the forest and using a crudely fashioned block of wood, stepped it onto the keel. Again using green spars, we rigged a small gaff mainsail. The sewing of the sail took us the most time, but it was pleasant work and we felt a rising excitement as we thought of our impending voyage. After adding a foresail, we had a neatly rigged vessel, fit to travel long distances. The new sails served very well as we tried them in the lagoon, and we were able to sail remarkably close to the wind. We would at least be able to choose the direction in which we escaped.

To complete our preparations, we loaded all the provisions we had been left, but we were deeply troubled by our lack of vessels in which to carry water. We searched for empty bottles and deeply regretted the ones we had smashed previously. We had our rum keg and sadly poured the rum into the sand to fill it with water. But the keg was small, not much over a gallon and a half, too small to supply us for more than a few days. Then there were coconuts and we filled the boat with them as being both food and drink.

To steer by, we had Long John's pocket compass and the directions in the Doctor's letter. It is true that a tropical voyage is less demanding that a similar trip in the waters around England, for the weather is normally much kinder. Only occasionally is there a great storm, and you might sail a lifetime without falling in with one of them. Anyway, we were confident that our natural wits would nearly suffice and youthful confidence would make up the difference. Our preparations for departure were nearly complete.

Our last duty on the island was to bury George and Johnny. We interred them in the pit where they had fallen, and at last gave the bones of Tom Allardyce a resting place with his old shipmates. Their grave is about two furlongs farther from the sea along the edge of the swamp. It was a large square hole and the three men lie there side by side. We felt sad as we took the path back to the beach for the last time. So many of the Walrus's crew had been buried on this unfortunate island, all seeking their fortunes and finding only their deaths.

As we rowed back to camp trailing a fishing line, we were lucky enough to catch several fat fish a little like herrings. We smoked them to take with us. As our tent cloth had already been used for sails, we spent our last night on the island under the stars. Neither of us slept well that night. We felt stirrings of nervousness in our stomachs. How would the journey turn out?

A Stormy Voyage

Next day dawned with a cloudless sky and a light breeze ruffling the sea. Impatient to be off we put our last belongings into the boat and set sail without eating. We would have time enough to eat the cold remains of last night's dinner once we were on our way. Before the sun had risen far, we were out of the shelter of the island and feeling a gentle deep-sea swell.

By the afternoon most of the island was out of sight; only the tip of the lookout hill remained above the horizon. There was something very unsettling in watching that familiar ground fall slowly behind. When you are at sea on a ship, with your friends beside you and a competent captain to take away the cares of navigation and sailing, there is a feeling of safety and normality. Matters were different with us. Our little boat was the only dry place in a very large and watery world. We did not know where we were and had only a vague idea of where we were going. Our first experience of the burdens of captaincy was not a comfortable one.

The breeze which had been bearing us and our cargo of coconuts and food across the ocean, died away as the day ended and our sails hung limp. The setting sun saw us drifting, so we furled the sails and curled up to sleep.

It must have been about the middle of the night when the movement of the boat woke us. The wind was getting up again and we hoisted sail to take advantage of it. Soon we were bowling along with a fine breeze on our quarter and the water slapping and hissing past the bottom of the boat. Even though we were making but a few knots (I could not guess how many), our nearness to the water gave us a feeling of great speed. This was not at all like watching the sea go past from the rail of a ship. It was an exciting way to travel.

At night, with stars lighting the great bowl of the sky like a church full of candles, we felt at home and at one with the world. Caspar held the lively tiller and kept course by the star falling to the west. Sleep slowly engulfed me.

How long I slept I do not know, but I was cruelly woken by being tipped into the bottom of the boat on top of the coconuts. I found I was lying in sea water. Caspar shouted at me to lower the mainsail and I hastened to obey, still groggy with sleep. In the dark and turmoil I cast off the halyard and, getting the boom on board, started to gather the folds of sail that filled the boat.

We had almost capsized. Caspar had been caught dozing and had only just managed to luff up as the gunwale went under. I took a pan and, much hindered by the coconuts which were floating inside the boat, started to bail. While I had been sleeping, the wind had freshened. The sea had risen now and as I struggled to empty the boat, spray from the bow splashed over us. For a while we drove on under the jib alone.

It was, I suppose, three o'clock in the morning. The warm tropical sea to which we had become accustomed was now taking on an aspect much more like our home waters. The wind and spray had soaked us through and we shivered with cold. Clearly the weather was worsening and we decided to heave to. Caspar brought her head to the wind and I brought down the jib.

After we had the sail safely stowed, we concentrated on bailing. The position was becoming very serious as the short seas slapped over the sides. The boat would not have much longer to live unless we could keep her head into the wind and lighten her load. I lashed our two oars together and dropped them over the side on the end of her painter as a sea-anchor. This helped. With her bows into the weather the inflow of water eased a little.

Rain now added to our misery. A heavy cloud-burst poured water like a stream from the sky. The weight of falling water at least had the effect of flattening the choppy sea, but we still could not make much headway with our bailing. No sooner did we think we were gaining that a larger wave than usual would undo our work. I had already thrown some coconuts over the side. Now we set to dispose of them all. We threw our precious cargo away without thought other than the relief of ridding ourselves of a millstone.

As suddenly as it had come the squall started to gentle. The rain petered out and the wind slackened. Slowly we dried the boat until it was riding easily to my makeshift sea-anchor. Now exhaustion set in. In our panic to stay afloat and alive, we had been spending more energy than we could afford. Now the bill must be paid. Trembling with cold we gathered our soaking clothes around us and lay down to sleep.

However, the weather had not yet done with us. We were woken by a loud hissing and roused ourselves. Dawn was near, already a grey light was spreading to the east, and the air felt cold and fresh. We scanned the flat sea for the source of the noise that had woken us. Coming towards us from the western dark was a massive black pillar, reaching upwards and out of sight. It was a waterspout. The winds had gathered themselves into a roaring chimney and were sucking water up from the sea. Water, sea-weed and fish are consumed by these monsters, sucked into the sky and dropped again when the wind's energy is dissipated. We would be destroyed if it touched us.

In a frenzy, we hauled on the painter to get our oars back. A few seconds struggling unsuccessfully with the lashing, and I took my knife to it. We bent to the oars and urged our boat away from the waterspout's course.

The spout rolled ponderously on but as if it contained some malevolent spirit, its course slowly turned towards us. We were filled with horror and redoubled our efforts, but as we turned so the waterspout also altered course to meet us. All our rowing was having the effect of hastening our meeting with that dreadful pillar. We fought to turn away from and reverse our progress. For agonising seconds we struggled but again the waterspout turned towards us and became bigger as it approached. An instant later the faint daylight was blotted out and our boat bucked like a young horse as the forces of nature struck it from all sides. As if by a great invisible hand, we were seized and set spinning like a top.

The roaring of the wind deafened us, and it tore at our clothes and hair. We clung to the boat as we were whirled round with increasing speed. I was clenched to the thwart, hugging myself close to its hardness. My oar had gone from my hand, but I did not recall dropping it. In the grip of such mighty forces we were helpless. My body was clinging to the boat and trying to breathe the water-laden air without choking. My spirit was elsewhere, but I can offer none of the thoughts I might have had in such a supreme moment.

I do not know how long our ordeal lasted. Maybe it was minutes or perhaps only seconds. It was brought to an abrupt end by a deluge of water crashing down on us, beating the breath out of our bodies. And then all was quiet.

By the Grace of God, we were alive. The sea lay flat and undisturbed around us in the growing dawn. The waterspout had gone, completely dissipated. Perhaps it had already been dying when its edge touched us. As it was, the water that had fallen around us had almost swamped the boat. The water inside our little vessel was almost at a level with the water outside. In a state of panic we started to bail by splashing the water out with our hands, which at least gave us time to collect our scattered wits and look about us. After the frenzy of the waterspout, the sea was completely calm. About us floated sea-weed and dead fish. Not even a swell disturbed the icy quietness of the sea's surface. Apart from ourselves and the sea-water, our boat appeared to contain nothing. The sails and yards had disappeared. The oars too had gone, and so had all of our provisions. I took off my shirt and using it between us like a scoop, we began to lower the water level perceptibly.

We had no time to consider our future. We considered only the task of the moment, which was to cast the water from the boat. As it dropped some blessings were slowly revealed. By some freak of fortune, our jib was still with us. Not in the boat, it was true, but by some lucky chance the sheet had become neatly wrapped around a thwart and it was now in the water alongside. A battered pan had been jammed into the stern, and that would help with the bailing. In the bow was a coconut, apparently wearing my old straw hat. Our axe and other tools were lying in the bottom of the boat. We had nothing else. Food and especially drink were going to be a problem.

We hoisted the jib and waited for the fitful breeze to move us on but by mid-morning it had dwindled to nothing, leaving our little boat pinned to the flat calm of the sea by a fierce sun overhead. The heat of the sun became oppressive and it was borne in on us that, without water, we could not hope to survive many days in these conditions.

We immediately started to take what steps we could. Caspar wished to fashion a spear and stood in the bows searching for a suitable shaft. In time he spotted a cane drifting a short way off, and we paddled using our hands and arms towards it. It was short and water-logged but by tying to it the blade of our bradawl, Caspar had a serviceable spear and hung over the bow looking for fish. I managed to pry a small nail from an old patch in the stern of the boat and fashioned from it a fishing hook. With a line made by unravelling my hat-band I dipped unsuccessfully for fish. The tranquillity that comes with fishing calmed us after the terror of the morning.

The sun sank into a fiery sea after a dry and hungry day. We had had no luck at our fishing and we lay down to sleep wrapped in our own thoughts. The next day brought the same unforgiving calm. We rigged the jib to give a little shade, and again we looked for food from the deep, without success. The day passed very slowly and we welcomed the coolness of the night. Our third day dawned and the sun sprang from the sea to begin its slow torment.

As the fierce heat of the day grew to its peak, we opened our coconut. What a blessed elixir it contained. True milk and honey slipped down our parched throats as we drank sip by sip, turn and turn about. We resolved not to break open the drained nut until the morrow. Caspar had given up trying to fish and sat in the bottom of the boat staring at nothing. His lowness bore me down too.

Already, after only three days, we were in a very bad way and suffering acutely from the sun. Although we dashed water over our heads, we seemed to get no relief, and we knew the drinking of sea-water would be fatal. We were crusted with salt and our lips were dry and cracked. It may surprise you that we were in such an extreme case so quickly, but the lack of water can kill rapidly. And any depression of the spirit will only accelerate the process.

The sun rose on a fourth day of misery. To celebrate it we opened the coconut and painfully ate our share of the flesh. Still no breath of wind brought relief. We were near to resigning ourselves to death, and Caspar had stretched out in the bottom of the boat, apparently unable to stay awake.

During the afternoon he became restless in his sleep, muttering and sighing. I sat in the stern, crushed by the unfairness of Providence. Soon Caspar would die, and then I would surely follow. If I could have found tears, I would have wept. The bronze sun fell into the sea, ending another day. In my extremity I prayed to God and then slept.

I was woken by rain. The stars had clouded over, there was a breeze, and tropical rain storm had started to fall. Soon the downpour was hissing into the sea around us. The cold water stirred Caspar, but he was already too weak to assist in my efforts to channel water off the jib and into our pan. I wasted precious moments pouring a quart of water into Caspar, and went back to filling our pan and drinking as much as I could of the overflow. As the storm started to die away, I had a full pan and a full stomach. In fact the effect of so much water after the drought gave me a cramp in my innards and I could only curl up and suffer.

It seemed, however, that other beings had been awakened by the rain. About us there were flurries in the water. Beneath its black surface, a struggle for life was taking place as silver prey fought to escape from their hunter. As I sat up to watch, something cold and alive struck me violently in the chest. A fish like a mullet fell from me into the bottom of the boat. For the space of two seconds we were under a silver arch as fish leapt from the water in a frenzy. Most flew over our boat in an arrow's curve. Some were cut short by slapping against the side. I instinctively reached out to catch them but I might as well have reached to the moon in a village pond. My hands passed through them as if through an illusion and the silver shower had gone. The sea lay quiet again, but slapping in the bottom of our boat were seven fat and bountiful fish.

The drink had revived Caspar and he was sitting and looking at me, but saying nothing. I diced one of our catch and fed him piece by piece.

I cannot recommend raw fish. It tastes of very little and is unpleasant to chew, but without having been starving you cannot imagine how wonderful it was.

The sun rose on a hopeful day. There were clouds in the sky and the breeze filled our small sail nicely. I dressed the fish and hung it to dry. The wind and sun would dry it very well and we would be fed for several days. I fed half a fish to Caspar. He felt a little stronger and managed a few words of conversation. He took small pieces of fish during the day, along with sips of water. By the day's end he had recovered enough to help me rig the sail to benefit from an evening thunderstorm. Again we were blessed with more fresh water than we could drink and went to sleep wet through but not thirsty.

What a blessed morn we woke to! Over our bow floated a heavy dark line on the horizon capped with a dressing of clouds. It could only be land. And as if to make amends the sea had yielded more food, a flying fish lying in the bottom of the boat.

In the middle of the night our boat ground up onto a white beach of shells and coral sand. We slept that night under the stars with opened coconuts beside us.

A Peaceful Haven

I woke to find we were being stared at. From the bushes that fringed the beach, some naked brown children were watching us. I smiled at them and they dissolved into shrieks of laughter, and then flew away like a flock of starlings. Shouting as they went they ran down the strand, the older ones leading and a fat little boy striving to keep up.

The beach the wind had chosen for us was a spit of sand running out to a rocky headland. The sandy ground behind the strand had been planted, amongst the wild palms and bushes, with many coconuts and breadfruit trees, presumably by the inhabitants of the village we could see at the other end of the beach. That end of the beach was sheltered by a substantial reef and the village houses came right down to the quiet waters of the lagoon. We could make out canoes pulled up onto the beach or stowed under the grass houses. We thanked God that we happened ashore where we did. Our boat would surely have been smashed if we had run onto the reef.

Anticipating visitors, we settled for a quick coconut breakfast and tidied up our boat. Soon enough, we saw a large procession of forty or fifty people coming towards us from the village. We prayed that they would be friendly.

The procession was led by a group of older men, presumably the Parish Council. The members of the council all wore skirts of long grass reaching to their knees, and apart from that, very little else. They had a promiscuous taste in ornament, all being adorned in necklaces of shells, bracelets of shell and chains of teeth. How fervently we prayed that the teeth were not human. (We need not have worried. We found out later that they were dogs' teeth.) Feathers were obviously much prized, either in necklaces or in the hair. The leader, much the oldest of the councillors, incongruously wore a shirt. Behind him, the other villagers were gathering, men and women, youngsters and many, many children. At the edges of the throng wandered dogs and small brown pigs. All the adults wore grass skirts and the men, not the women, wore what jewellery there was. None of them, however, approached the elegance of the man on whom our attention was fixed.

The headman was well past his prime. His limbs were wasted by age and his hair was thin and grey. He addressed us first, in no recognisable language, and then everyone tried speaking to us. Quickly realising that we were too ignorant to understand, they fell to examining our hair, our clothes and our fair skin. Our boat was also of great interest, but the crowd's attention was mostly drawn to the iron tools lying in its bottom. The headman seized our adze and with unmistakable gestures asked that we should give it to him.

We were at their mercy, but they were disposed to be friendly. I proposed to use the headman's desire for iron tools to our advantage. By mime I explained our need for food and drink, and sailcloth, and oars. If he could find these things for us, we would give him not only the adze but the saw and chisels as well. The curious hands reaching for our tools were stopped at once. With great harshness he ordered some women back to the village, and set others to making a fire. He and the rest of the men sat down to wait.

Caspar still felt desperately weak, and I was not feeling too strong, so we were glad of the opportunity to sit down. The headman, whose name we found was Aman, was accorded great respect by all his companions. He sat on a palm leaf (cut with our adze) and enjoyed a yard or so of breathing space all round. As honoured guests, we basked in the same deference. So we sat, whisking away the flies that gathered on us and our new friends.

Aman fell to comparing our fair skins to his own mahogany colour, and remarking on the colour of our eyes. He held his forearm alongside mine and displayed to his companions the contrast between our colours. The people of the village were of an Indian type with strong black hair, which they wore long. They were curious to touch ours (mine was fair and curly then). On our side, we wanted to know the way to Port Domingo. We kept repeating the name and pointing along the coast in what we believed was the right direction, but we were rewarded only by puzzled faces.

I tried to mime Port Domingo and after (I cannot imagine how) I had conveyed the idea of a very large village with many boats, a stocky young man suddenly shouted "P'tomingu, P'tomingu!" All of a sudden everyone was laughing and shouting, just as for a Christmas parlour game. Aman confidently told us it was many, many days away (he rendered days by pointing at the sun and bringing it up out of the eastern sea and then down again behind the forest). No one actually contradicted him but the stocky young man, seated behind Aman and out of his sight, pointed at our boat and then held up two fingers and cut a third in half. Maybe he had travelled there himself.

Now they wanted to know where we had come from, and I had to explain that England was several months away to the east, and that it was cold with little sun and no coconuts. In the sand I drew a picture of a ship.

I found they were familiar with them. I suppose ships passed by the point en route to Port Domingo every week. As we talked, we watched the women returning bearing food and pots. The others already had several small fires going.

It was a pleasure to watch the women and girls set to work boiling yams and sweet potatoes, breadfruit and plantains, grilling fresh fish over the fire and stirring a rich soup which contained fish heads, peppers and coconuts at least. They laid the food was before us on newly cut banana leaves, and the dark shiny green of our makeshift plates displayed the food like a banquet. Aman and the guests of honour (us) were served the choicest parts of a small pig the men had butchered and set over the fire still warm. The meal made a royal feast for two half-starved sailors accustomed to nothing better than ship's biscuit and salt pork. Our hosts insisted on our eating to the point of discomfort, and they did the same themselves.

Such a huge meal and the hot afternoon sun combined to send us to sleep, and most of our hosts with us. Men and women curled up on the sand and slept unashamed and unafraid. We needed no consideration of politeness to make us join them.

I awoke when the sun was already falling into the forest behind us. Most of our friends were also awake, sitting in small groups chattering quietly or watching the children run up and down the beach, splashing in and out of the edge of the sea. Some of the women had stoked up a fire, and seeing me awake, hastened to bring food and drink. The day of our arrival had been taken as an excuse for a holiday, and apart from cooking no one had done anything that could be called work. All that remained was to round the day off with singing and dancing. A group of women sitting in a circle started to sing and clap. The tune was strange and the words were foreign, but the effect was very fine for all that. When the men joined in, the music was as good as any you might hear in church on Sunday. After two or three songs, Aman called out a command and shyly at first, all the women except the very young and the very old got up to dance. They stood in a long line and sang, accompanying themselves by clapping and stamping their feet. Facing first one way and then another, they swayed to the music dancing more and more energetically as the men beat out the time and shouted the words of the song.

Smiling and elated, the women sat down and a young man took their place. His dance, so Aman told us, was an imitation of a bird, either a sea-bird or perhaps an eagle (it was hard to guess from the old man's gestures). The music was given by drums and singing, from the men alone. We had to do a turn as well. Caspar was far too weak to manage his hornpipe, so I had to do my best, singing and dancing at the same time. The drummers soon picked up the rhythm and it was, I suppose, the strangest hornpipe you ever saw. I am afraid it ended by my tripping over my feet and pitching into the sand, which probably gave my audience more pleasure than the dance itself for they rolled on the sand and laughed until they were in pain. Honour matched, we sat down to watch more songs and dances until Aman stood up. We politely refused his invitation to sleep in his hut and elected to sleep where we were, along with several of the party who stayed out of companionship or perhaps because they considered their homes were too far away to walk back.

The night was mild and quiet, and we were lulled by the gentle lapping of the sea against the sand. For all that, sleep was slow in coming because I had done little more than rest all day, so I lay watching the stars climb the great bowl of the sky until my eyelids finally closed.

The next day was for business. Aman did not come himself but sent a small party of women bearing a mat woven out of some kind of flat dried leaf. This, they demonstrated, would be our sail and they had come to trim it with thin ropes made from the same dried leaves. I hastened to cut a boom (our old spars having been taken by the waterspout) and showed them how I wanted to secure the sail to the mast and boom. I need not have worried. Sail making was a skill that belonged to women here. My team of sail makers made an amazing sight. They were all pretty brown ladies wearing nothing but grass skirts, and for ornament, flowers in their hair. They spread the sail on the sand and knelt to their work.

With Caspar watching over the sail makers, I turned my attention to the oars we needed. The natives of those parts do not use oars, preferring paddles for their canoes, and it proved difficult to obtain dry poles of the right dimensions. Eventually two were brought from the village and cutting the handles from two paddles, I proceeded to pin them to the poles with wooden pegs. This drew interest and approval from the men who had gathered to watch. I showed one of them how I wanted the handles shaped and he set to with my knife to give them smooth handles that did not give me a single blister when I later came to use them.

As the oars neared completion, so did the sail. The ladies watched it hoisted, but took it down again for correction. When it was finally ready and hoisted on the mast, they stood admiring it and chattering with animation. Their leader, rather more matronly in her figure than her helpers, warned us firmly not to use the sail if it was thoroughly wet. It must first be hung to dry before any strain was put on it.

As the day ended, our boat was ready for sea again, and we had more hospitality to enjoy. We were led to the village, to the house of Aman, where we would have another party. After night had fallen, the entire village, including pigs, dogs and chickens, gathered in front of Aman's house and sat on the ground in a rough circle. This time there were more drums and flutes, more dance and more songs. On the hard beaten earth the primitive dances were more vigorous, and the pounding of bare feet more insistent and hypnotic. The food was good and limitless, and to accompany it came a form of beer made from coconuts. Again I danced the hornpipe, earning generous applause and laughter, together with requests to fall down again. Seeing we had become impossibly sleepy, Aman's children led us by the hand up the rickety ladder into the house. There on the floor we fell asleep to the beat of the dancing drums.

In the morning, we were taken in procession by the entire village back to our boat. The day had dawned clean and fresh and there was a breeze to carry us away. Willing hands hauled the boat down the sand to get us afloat, and stowed aboard enough food and water to cross an ocean. Then, as our sail began to draw, all the women stood in a swaying line at the water's edge and gave us one last song. Their graceful gestures and the mournful sadness of the song could easily have turned us around and kept us there for the rest of our lives. Their singing carried across the water after us as we rounded the point.

Port Domingo

The rising sun picked out the houses of Port Domingo far away across the bay. We were in no great hurry to arrive and so did not trouble to row. We preferred to idle away the time until the land breeze picked up, fishing a little and talking. We had been remarkably silent between ourselves since we left the treasure island. It seemed the tribulations we had suffered had borne down upon us and driven us to look inside ourselves. However, our young bodies were recovering rapidly and Caspar was regaining his vigour.

Caspar recalled the good times he had known while following the trade of soldier. He had gone away young, little more than a boy, marching along the Downs after a recruiting sergeant. He had liked the life that he described as not much different from shipboard, with regular duties and a good company of men of all sorts. Before he had really learnt to use his musket or had time to build up his manly strength, he had shipped off to the Low Countries to take part in wars there.

He had not fought in any great battles but had participated in skirmishing. Most of his days were spent marching from place to place as the generals ordered. He and his companions, all country men, stared and stared at the foreign ways of doing things, of growing corn, harnessing horses, draining the land, planting and harvesting. All through a long and sunny summer, his regiment trailed the highways and by-ways of the Low Countries and Caspar grew fit and brown.

He told of a time when he and a few others were billeted in a walled garden for a while. One afternoon they had all sat in the sun with their backs to the wall, listening in the stillness to the bees at their work and drinking champagne looted from a great house. It was their first taste of such a heady drink and very pleasant they found it. They fell asleep like leaves falling into a still pool, not insensible because they had not drunk enough for that, but just washed away by the heavy stillness of the summer air. The whole group of them slept against that sunny wall until the evening trumpets woke them and sent them scurrying after tasks that should have been completed long ago.

Caspar's tales of the doings of Sergeant This and Trooper That, and of the fine fellowship of his regiment on the march, brought us to the harbour mouth of Port Domingo. As we looked inside we saw an unwelcome sight. Moored several cables off-shore lay a king's ship. The sharp, clean lines of her hull were picked out in black and cream paint, and her prodigiously gilt figurehead depicting some species of sea-nymph stared superciliously at us as we rowed below her. All the ports of her two gun decks stood open for the breeze to pass through, and her guns had been run out to give space to the men we could see passing to and fro in the shaded darkness. We remembered the small pouches of silver we carried against our skins and hoped she knew nothing of us or the Hispaniola. As we approached the landing, a launch rounded her stern and pulled for the shore.

What an elegant sight that launch made, freshly painted and uniform, even to the matching oar-blades dipping in unison. She was crewed by eight solid-looking sailors clad in clean white duck frocks and straw hats, their tarred pigtails hanging down their backs. In the stern sat a severe officer, his hat a blaze of gold lace, and beside him a midshipman. They swept past us in a rush towards the landing.

"Now there's a fine way to travel!" mused Caspar as he stared after them.

It was a little time before we crept alongside the launch to the accompaniment of various imprecations and warnings to keep clear of her paintwork. The officer had gone ashore and the midshipman stood on the quay with one sailor. I made our painter fast and, leaving Caspar to mind the boat, went off to find Bewley the chandler and, hopefully, Long John's hiding place.

Bewley's was a dark labyrinth that opened directly onto the quay. Here, piled at random, lay everything a sea-faring man might want for his ship. Tubs of nails, blocks and dead-eyes, cordage of all dimensions, galley-pans, various weights of chain, cleats, shackles, paint, pitch, linseed oil, copper sheet, gilt for the gingerbread, patent polish and a brass cannon to go with it, hammocks ready-made, quadrants for tiller ropes, knives for the sailors, sextants and telescopes for the officers, oil-skins, fine hats, eyelets, sailcloth, tarpaulin, salt pork, salt fish, salt itself, fish-hooks for tiddlers or shark, harpoon blades and boat-hooks. A cornucopia, a lexicon of supplies. And if you cared to pass on through to the yard behind, you would find timbers, planks, spars, tuns, anchors galore.

Scampering in and out of these wares were several clerks, all looking more or less respectable but inevitably hot and dusty. I stopped one.

"Is Mr. Bewley here?"

He looked me over quickly. "No. What do you want?"

"I want to speak with Mr. Bewley. I don't want anything."

The clerk snorted. "I'll see if he's here." Without haste he disappeared.

I stood for a while bemused by the material around me, trying to identify everything I saw. I had to crane my neck to make out the items hanging in the darkness of the ceiling.

"He wants to know your business," the clerk had reappeared.

"Tell him Mr. Gold sent me," I said.

Within moments he returned and beckoned to me. "He's in the office up the stairs." I mounted the steep stairway hidden at the back of the store. Passing upwards I could stare at the layers of goods stored on shelves or suspended from pillars or the ceiling. Near the top of the staircase was a window in the wall, opening onto a small landing, placed so the whole store could be surveyed. Through it I could peep into the office of the chandlery. Two clerks were working on ledgers at high tables but, standing in front of them and looking straight back at me, was a stout man with wispy hair. He examined me for a moment, and motioned me onwards to the door.

This was Mr. Bewley, a severe and apparently upright man of business. He wasted no time before questioning me. "What's your name, boy? And where are the others?"

I gave my name and told of Caspar waiting with the boat. "And Mr. Morgan? Where would he be?" Bewley obviously had our full story.

"Dead. He died of a poisoned leg. He didn't come."

"No. I suppose he didn't. And now you want me to give you a shirt before you go and visit Mr. and Mrs. Gold, is that right?"

I looked down at the remnants of my shirt, scarcely enough to cover my back. There was something about Mr. Bewley's assumption of superiority that annoyed me. "Yes. I want a shirt. Do you have a good cotton one?"

Aware that he had pricked me, he laughed. "Certainly we do, a good cotton shirt, and cheap enough too." He opened the window and called for Clem.

"Clem will get you fitted up, and Mr. Gold's credit is good. Now, I'll have him show you the boatyard to leave your boat. Then he'll drive you to Mr. Gold's place, but you'll have to walk the last mile or so."

I left Bewley's wearing a new shirt and carrying another for Caspar, both paid for with my silver. I stood on the quayside looking down in surprise, for our little boat was empty. Clem, the bent little old man who would convey us to Long John, soon heard from one of the loafers on the wharf that Caspar had gone off in the Naval launch but that he had "written something on the seat,". I jumped down to the boat and found in charcoal the following note.

Dear Dick,

I have gone to join the big ship. I do not want to go back to the old trade, and I hope you will come too,

Your Friend Caspar

Caspar must have been tired of wandering and I believe he was hankering for a home. I looked across the water at the frigate, deadly but beautiful. Men were working all over her—in the rigging, on the deck, on stages over her sides. Caspar would certainly not be short of companions. Pretty as she looked, she was not the ship for me. I could get along very well without a bo'sun's cane to start me. It was a sad thing to lose my last comrade, but I would not join him.

Clem seated himself at the tiller and I rowed him round to the boatyard, one of Mr. Bewley's enterprises that built and repaired small coasters. Here we left the trusty little boat that had brought me so far, and set off for Mr. Bewley's stables. Clem turned out to be a very dashing whip and soon spun me off through the town and into the gardens beyond. The dusty road dived into the shadows of the coconut plantations interspersed with patches of forest and occasional villages of grass houses. Clem let the horses walk and we had a very comfortable journey. After some miles the road climbed a little way off the coastal flats and started to wind this way and then that through fields of giant grass. This was sugar cane, the gold mine of the rich planters. Sugar cane is indeed a grass, but with a heavy fibrous stem where the plant stores its sugar. This stem, or cane, is an inch or more in thickness and will grow higher than a man. We cut a ripe one and chewed the sugary sap out of short lengths as we went along.

The road wound gently down through more coconuts as we again approached the sea. Clem drew the horses up. "Here, now. Take the path there, all the way down to the beach. Keep the sea on your right hand and walk along the beach. You'll pass some rocks and then there'll be a long, long strand with a big house set back a bit. That's where you're going. You can't mistake it. It's alone and the gardens come right down to the sea." As I started down the path I heard him touch the horses into a trot.

It was easy to feel light-hearted that day, notwithstanding Caspar's sudden departure. The sea gently beat on the strand beside me, and the light afternoon breeze kept any biting insects away. From the coconut plantation I had shade, and there was an easy path of beaten earth to guide me. Believe me, those island beaches must be the prettiest, pleasantest places on earth, a fore-taste of Paradise.

My path led to a low, rocky headland two miles or more away. I hurried on, eager to see Long John again and give him my news. I was imagining how I would string my tale together when the most remarkable thing occurred, the most remarkable in my life before or since. My path drew near to the rocks and turned inland to pass behind them. As it returned towards the sea, I walked through dense natural undergrowth, in the deep shadow of the forest. I could hear the sea, and above it childish voices at play. The shadow was dispelled at the edge of the beach and there, alone on the sand, a picture framed by the trees and with the blue sea beyond, sat the most beautiful girl in the world.

She was watching some children in the water, Creole children, and combing her long black hair that fell in waves almost to the sand. She wore a piece of brightly coloured material wrapped around her, leaving her arms and shoulders bare. Somehow conscious that she was being watched, she turned and far from starting up in fright, she smiled. How shall I describe her? Delicate features, mantled by the waves of her black hair. Sharp, sparkling eyes drawn tight by her wide smile. White, white teeth. No, it is no good. My pen will not carry the picture onto the paper.

I found myself reaching to remove a hat I was not wearing and mumbling "Good morning," like a shepherd suddenly brought before the Queen of England. She giggled at me, and I sidled rapidly off along the path feeling I had been struck by lightning.

Another corner, and a long white beach opened up before me. A fair distance along it there was a break in the trees and, as Clem had described it, a large house set back from the beach. There were lawns of short grass leading up to it, and very old, very tall palms stood scattered around. The house was built of wooden boards painted white, and carried on short stumps to aid in the circulation of the breeze and to discourage creeping pests. It was large and low, one storey high, with a steep thatched roof. A deep shaded verandah ran all around and on it sat the Lord of the Manor, Long John Silver himself.

I ran up the steps to a joyful greeting. Long John was a study in relaxed elegance—fawn breeches with silver buckles, silk stocking, and a loose muslin shirt. He was far removed from anyone's picture of a pirate captain. He sat me down and laughed off my questions about the grandeur of his surroundings. "Just a little place I was keeping up for when I'm done with the sea." That was all the explanation he would give. He had heard of our finding the silver from Doctor Livesey and wanted to know more. He was also keen to hear about my journey, and about Chips and Caspar.

Chips he dismissed as a bit old and a little unlucky, no help for it. Caspar was another matter. "There's only two of you know about the silver," he said, "and who's to say that Caspar won't let out the story? He's got silver about him and they'll be asking him where it came from, sure as daylight. His mates will have the story out of him eventually, then that old Captain'll hear, and I'll lay to it that he'll find some excuse to put in and water or something-like, and stumble over it all accidental. We'd better ship out smartish or we shall be too late." He laughed. "Here you are, hardly set foot on dry land and I'm shipping you off again. No. That won't do. You'll stop here for maybe a week while I get everything ready."

Just at that moment, Sally came onto the verandah bearing a tray with glasses of lime juice. "Welcome, Dick, welcome!" She drew up a chair and waved me back into mine. "Did you have a good trip?" I was taken aback. Not only Long John fitted into these opulent surroundings but Sally too was every inch a lady. These were her natural surroundings and she was at home.

"Why did you walk along the beach? You would have saved yourself a long walk if you had come on with Clem."

Long John coughed and looked embarrassed. "That's just Bewley's way, my dear. Clem came on ahead to make sure everything was ready."

"Stupid man!" Sally muttered and sipped her lime juice. "Will you be staying long?"

Long John answered for me. "I think we'll be taking a little trip, my dear. About a week or two, starting next week."

"Oh, no!" Sally was cross. "You've only been back a week! And it's so boring when you're not here." She flung herself back in her chair and stared at the ceiling in silence.

"Come on, Sally. Don't take on so. We'll only be gone for a few days. You'll hardly notice it."

But Sally would not be mollified. "Well, if you must go, I suppose I shall just have to be patient." She strutted off into the house, showing very little likelihood of being so.

Long John looked flustered. "Well now. I shall just have to talk her round to it. She'll like the idea better when she hears of the silver. Tell me about it. How much was there?"

He listened carefully to my story, asking questions here and there. He approved of our burying our old shipmates and wished them well. He congratulated me on our voyage and especially on our lucky escape from the waterspout. "You were almost done for there, my lad. Almost joined the fishes. Now what did Caspar go running off like that for? After being so lucky, an' all."

I explained I thought it had more to do with finding a new ship and a home than anything else. "Oh, well. He'll have that, surely. The Royal Navy will take good care of him, when they aren't flogging him or letting the Spaniards blow him up.

"Now then, we shall have to find you a place to sleep. And some clothes, I suppose. Clem left your spare shirt that you'd forgotten. I don't suppose you have anything else, no? No matter, we don't shift our clothes for dinner here. I don't hold with that sort of foolishness. Better to be what you are than to pretend to be something else, that's what I say."

I returned to the verandah as the sun was falling into the sea. I was freshly washed, and wearing my clean shirt and borrowed breeches. "Well, now! Ain't you a sight!" Long John was stretched back in his chair. "Here, sit down and have some punch." The punch was made of fruit juice and rum, and slipped down very sweetly.

We watched in silence as the last rim of the sun slipped away. As the tropic night fell, Long John sighed. "This is the life for me, Dick my lad. I'm home for keeps. Hanging up my oil-skins and turning into a farmer. I've no call to go running around the sea at my age."

I laughed at him. "You'll never leave the sea. What are you going to do with yourself? You've already said we'll be sailing again next week."

"Now that's true. And so we shall. But it's the last time. Look, I don't have so much as a jolly boat, not even to do a spot of fishing. I'll have to borrow one for this trip. No, when I get back, I'm staying on land. This wooden leg of mine will sprout leaves before I go to sea again."

I could hear a female voice approaching singing a hymn familiar in words but strangely sung. "Dinner will be ready soon, Mr. John." called the owner of the voice from the doorway, presumably a Creole servant from her sing-song accent. "I'm just going to light the candles."

"Well enough, Mary. We'll come along now. Come on, Dick, and bring your punch with you. Sally will have me sit down and eat properly at least once a day."

The dining room was small, with windows opening onto the verandah. The white tablecloth and the candlelight glinting off the service made for a regal appearance. The elegance of the setting was torn apart by the entry of the food, borne by Sally and the cook. It was a pepper-pot with rice, typical of Sally's cooking. Diced meat in a fiery red sauce ladled onto a bed of rice, it had a smell of exquisite richness.

"Sit down, Dick," she said, her recent upset apparently forgotten. "Sit down and I'll serve you. Where's Isabel? Maria, go and call Isabel."

No sooner had the cook left the room than there appeared standing in the doorway—the girl from the beach! I stopped with my glass halfway to my lips. Gone was the wild beauty from the sea-shore and in her place was a fashionable young lady in a dress of white lace. Her hair was done up into a top-knot, making her elegant neck seem even longer. She had no jewellery save small gold earrings, and needed none. She glided into the room in silence until her mother caught sight of her.

"Look at the fine lady!" said Sally with approval.

"Oh, Mother!" Isabel's facade vanished like smoke, and she was a girl again.

"Come on, girl, sit down. There, next to Dick. Dick, this is Isabel. Do you remember her? Dick is one of your father's friends."

"I've seen you before," I blundered. "You were on the American Providence when we all sailed to Bristol. But you were only a girl then."

Long John laughed at me. "That was not so much over a year ago, Dick. Not so much at all. Hasn't she come on well? She's a proper woman now, just like her mother."

It takes a great deal of patience to put up with comments like that from your parents, but Isabel managed to keep her balance then and throughout the meal.

Treasure Hunting Again

There now started a very happy period in my life. Long John's sugar plantation lay free for me to roam in, and Isabel was the most delightful guide. While Long John went to town to make the arrangements for our trip, she (with a servant for propriety's sake) led me to every corner of the estate, and showed me every local beauty spot. We visited the field workers in their gangs and accompanied their children to the beach. We rode up the coast to visit friends or we paddled a canoe over the glass world of the reefs. Sally seemed happy to leave Isabel in my hands and made sure only that we returned early enough for dinner.

Isabel made a lively companion and seemed to enjoy her position as my guide. She was completely charming when she chose to be, and I suppose she led me around by the nose. After all, I was only a helpless youth and her hold over me increased daily. In her careless racing way, she seemed to accept that as normal. However, she made no gesture of affection towards me.

I suppose it was some four or five days after I had arrived that we attended the wedding celebrations of one of the chambermaids. At Sally's insistence, an Irish priest came from town and the service took place in the open near the workers' cabins. It was a good service that every living thing on the estate attended, right down to the scrawny chickens. The workers, mostly Negroes, were enthusiastic choristers and their singing was a real, joyful celebration before God. Isabel and I stood in the congregation watching the bride and groom being joined together. I do not know what she was thinking about, but to my surprise, I found my thoughts about her had advanced very far indeed. I had fallen in love for the first and only time in my life.

A dinner followed the wedding, and then dancing to the wild, wild beat of the Negro drums. Everybody danced and even Long John stood at the edge of the circle tapping his toes and clapping out the rhythm. I was induced to dance with a line of field hands making movements that had to do (I think) with warriors fighting in their native continent.

As I stood enjoying the spectacle, Isabel brought a leg of chicken and offered it to me with a smile. She looked so beautiful that my heart turned upside down, and turned again when she whispered, "Go down to the beach and wait for me."

Suddenly I felt as out of place as a bull in a church. I am sure my efforts to dissimulate were laughable, and it was fortunate that everyone was so occupied. I strolled to the edge of the firelight and paused to see if anyone was watching. Nobody seemed to have noticed so I slipped away and hurried to the beach.

On the short grass behind the beach I sat looking out over the sea. The night was still, and the sparkling silver road to the full moon stretched smooth away from me. The party behind the house sounded as if from the far distance.

With the slightest rustle Isabel appeared at my side, giving me her hand. "Come over here." Her hand felt small, warm and dry. We moved to the shadows of a young palm where we stood out of sight of the house, still holding hands. My heart raced within me and I did not know what to do, or what to expect.

She turned to face me. "Dick, do you like me?" I am sure I mumbled something about my feelings for her, for she smiled and squeezed my hand. "Wait here a while before you go back," she said, and raced off.

I was storm-tossed and in a turmoil. I did go back to the party and wandered around the dancers without joining in, but all the time my spirit flew elsewhere. I could still feel the pressure of her hand as she left, and I was racked with uncertainty as to what her behaviour signified. Was she fond of me or not? You may be sure I slept little that night.

Next morning early Sally took her daughter to town, and I was left to mope about the estate by myself. Long John did not return that day and I dined alone. He appeared about noon of the next day. He strode into the dining room and shouted for luncheon. "I've got something for you, Dick my lad. Just let me get some vittles and we'll go and have a look at her."

Long John had brought the boat in which we would travel back to the island. It was tied up in the small creek that served the estate as a port, and field hands were busy getting water and other essentials aboard. I suppose the boat was of the type known as a ketch because it had two masts as a ketch should. However she looked very small, not over thirty feet in length, and the mizzen mast looked a very stumpy affair. She had obviously been built for work rather than speed.

"So, Dick. I'll be captain and you'll be mate. What do you think of that?"

I was thinking that even a little boat would sail more smoothly with a bit of a crew on board and asked if we might take a couple of boys with us. They would come in handy to help with the silver if nothing else. But Long John would have nothing of it. "I don't want no one from round here knowing what's afoot, Dick. Or we might wake up one fine morning with our throats cut. We sail tomorrow and maybe we'll pick up a couple of hands from Domingo."

The boat had been borrowed or hired from Bewley, and had previously been used as a coaster. The hold was in ballast only, though the smell made it evident that the last cargo had been dried fish. I set about a real mate's duties of rousing out the sails, knotting and splicing, stowing the victuals and generally getting to know where everything was. Dark had come before I felt anything like ready to sail. Isabel had not returned, and it seemed I would sail without seeing her. I comforted myself that we would not be away long.

Next morning Long John and I poled out into the creek and let the current carry us towards the sea. As we cleared the trees a gentle breeze swung the boom firmly against the sheet and we were off. Long John had the tiller and I scampered around trimming sails and stowing cables. We stood along the coast to Port Domingo, leaving the house to hide in its palm trees.

As we came up to the port, we saw a small boat towing another rowing out of the harbour. Long John steered us towards it and I could see that it carried, in addition to the two Negroes at the oars, Sally and Isabel. The towed boat was another old friend, the one that had brought me from the island. The two men dropped off their charges and rowed away. It seemed we were to have a female crew for the voyage.

Of course, female company is a very fine thing but on a boat it is perhaps less welcomed than one might expect. In fact, women on board a ship are generally held to be unlucky, and it is certain that the presence of one or two women can upset a male crew with jealousy and dissension. I was afraid that two passengers would add to my work, but I need not have worried. This was far from Sally's first voyage and she immediately took over the galley. Her cooking skills, supplemented by the dainties she had thought to bring along, made for a most luxurious voyage.

Isabel had no duties and had only to help her mother, leaving the rest of her time free for chattering to the helmsman, fishing, or sleeping in the shadow of the jib.

Return to the Island

In the short time I had been away from our island, the jungle had already started its work of covering the site of the silver. Creepers twined in the brushwood cover, and the young trees around it seemed to lean in to shade the spot. Uncovering the treasure was left to me, with Sally and Isabel waiting eagerly for the first sight. When it came and I had with difficulty levered the first keg up to ground level, it was difficult to prevent their opening it. Only the promise of being able to see inside the broken one won their co-operation and they started to roll the keg towards the beach.

Unearthing the kegs proved much more difficult than burying them and I felt deeply tired before we fought the last one up over the lip of the hole. Then came the work of carrying them down to the beach, rolling them having proved too much for the ladies. It was late in the afternoon before we had them on board the ketch and safely stowed. What a comfortable feeling that was! After all the toil and trouble, all the miles we had sailed and the friends we had lost, we had a ship of our own with an earl's ransom stowed below decks. We gratefully ate the mess of rice, bacon and peas that Long John had prepared, and toasted each other in coconut grog.

Long John had rigged an awning over the boom, giving us shade to lounge and eat our food. It also hid the sight of our nemesis creeping up behind us.

Something unaccountable caused me to stand up and look out to sea. To look out at the beautiful and terrifying sight of a man o' war reducing sail as she bore up on the other side of the reef. She had come so close we could hear the calls of the leadsman as she sought safe ground in which to anchor.

Horror struck us dumb. This was the frigate that Caspar had joined and her presence here could mean only one thing, our treasure was at risk again. We turned again to Long John.

"So. King George himself. We shall have to look sharp to get away now. I believe I shall stay where I am," (he was reclining on the deck) "Isabel, you stop here as well. Sally, take my hat and pipe and go and look at the ship all natural-like."

It was fortunate that the ladies still wore their treasure digging clothes. In her man's shirt and topped off with Long John's hat, Sally could pass at a distance for one of the island seamen. We stood in full view discussing the ship, Sally gesturing with her pipe. Need I say that in reality our stomachs trembled at the thought of the spy-glasses that were surely trained on us? We wanted to rush the sails up and run.

"Just stop where you are," commanded Long John. "Wait until she's settled in, then we'll see."

The ship dropped her anchor and furled her sails all in a rush. Her rigging and decks swarmed with sailors hurrying about their work, urged on by the shouts of their officers.

"Now if we just stay here and don't do nothing, there's a chance she won't take us for no more than what we are—just a coaster. Are they watching us?"

Several figures on the poop did seem to be studying us, and two had spy-glasses. Certainly the Captain did not waste any time for a party of sailors was busy swinging out a launch. Long John decided to move.

"Now, Dick and Isabel, get forward and pull that anchor. Sally, bear a hand here and we'll get this main up."

With an efficiency born of sheer fright we set to our tasks, trying all the while to appear unconcerned and unhurried. In short measure we gathered way, sheeting home the sails and casting anxious glances over our stern. The ship's launch, with two gleaming officers in the stern, pulled towards the beach, banks of white oar-blades sweeping her forward in measured strokes.

Providence or the hand of God was with us that day for the launch ran ashore right at the point, some distance from the path we had taken into the jungle.

"The fox will be in the hen-coop when they find your marks, Dick. Give me the tiller."

The wind, such as it was, lay a little forward of our port beam, and we were taking advantage of the shelter of the reef to run north towards the tip of the island. Long John kept busy coaxing the last fraction of a knot that he could from our boat, and he kept me equally busy trimming sheets and halyards to get the sails just so.

Long John grunted. "Don't matter if they find your marks now or later. I believe we shall weather that point on this tack, which is more than they ever will. And I'll lay that was the Captain that went ashore."

Back on shore, the officers had been carried dry-shod to the sand and set off with their men to walk along the beach. Presumably Caspar was there, guiding the party. The straggling group moved unhurriedly down the beach, stopping to pick up shells or to point out sights in the trees. Then they reached the marks of our passage and clustered around them.

Now we were for it, I thought, as the officers strode up. A quick look at the marks and they began looking at us and pointing. The group suddenly broke up and with an awful purpose started to run back to the launch, leaving only one officer and a man to check for the silver. The launch crew ran her out and tumbled aboard. Soon they were pulling hard after us, bent on our capture.

We looked in dismay at the wave being thrown up by the launch's bow. We were already more than a mile ahead and still gaining a little speed in a freshening breeze. However we had no doubt in our minds that, given time, the launch would catch us. However, there is a saying at sea that a stern chase is a long chase, meaning that chasing someone from directly behind is a long and slow business, and you must appreciate that we were not tiring ourselves out as the rowers were.

The launch did not waste strength in a senseless dash, but settled down to a long steady pull. Long John had a worried look on his face. "This ain't right. This is foolishness. Dick, load my pistols and the muskets."

When I got back on deck the launch looked nearer. The white oar blades dipped and rose in deadly unison. The pursuit had a sense of inevitability about it, and from Sally and Isabel's drawn faces I could see they were terrified.

"Ah, the Captain's coming back." Back on the beach, the two who had gone to check on the burial site had returned to the beach, the officer waving his handkerchief as he walked. His wishes must have been anticipated for a jolly boat was already pulling to meet him. The ship had pulled up towards her anchor, ready to get under way at the shortest of notice. Sure enough, as soon as the Captain was back on his quarter-deck, the sails began to fall and fill. Being square-rigged, she could not lie anywhere as near to the wind as we could, so she headed out to sea on the other tack. For the moment anyway she would be drawing away from us, but only to sweep back down faster than we could sail. But we would have to deal with the launch long before we had to worry about the frigate.

The launch gained on us steadily. The gold lettering on her bow was clear to read, and we could see the men's pig-tails slapping on their backs as they lent forward for each stroke. Still they came on, eating up the light green sea between us fathom by fathom.

Long John gave me the tiller and stood up. "Launch ahoy! Don't come no nearer or I'll shoot!"

His warning had no effect. "'Tis a wonderfully difficult thing to row backwards into trouble, Dick. I've tried it and it don't serve. You watch." He laid his pistol on the rail and called out, "I'm going to shoot." We could see no response to his call, so he squeezed the trigger.

140

The sound of the shot, if not the passing ball, brought the officer to his feet. He was a youngster, a midshipman I suppose, but as brave as a cock. With his hat tucked under his arm he stood firm and shouted back, "Fire if you will, pirate!"

"D--- him!" Long John took a musket. "I shall have to drop him now." It took a long moment before he was satisfied with his aim and had allowed for the movement of our boat. Choosing his moment, he fired. A true shot, and the officer fell back into the water clutching at his thigh. As he went, the rhythm of the rowers was upset. Someone threw an oar after the drowning man, and all was confusion. As they got the boat turned and rescued the officer, the gap between us widened rapidly.

"Good. That stopped them without too much harm done." Long John turned to watch the frigate and the ladies came up to link arms with him.

"Is she going away?" asked Isabel.

"No, my dear, she ain't. She'll be heading back for us just as soon as she's made her offing. But we can hurry along inside the reef and she'll have to go the long way round, all the way to the other side of the island. And by then it will be dark, so we'll see if we can't give her the slip."

"Look!" Sally pointed at the launch. They had got the young officer back on board and were rowing after us again, with half a mile or more to make up. Like a monstrous insect, the launch crawled in our wake. We turned back to our sails.

It may be that the wind was getting stronger or perhaps the rowers had begun to tire, for it seemed that the launch did not draw up as quickly as the last time. But draw up it did until the creak and splash of the oars mingled loudly with the sounds of our passage. We could see the crew straining and it became obvious that they would be unable to find the extra speed to rush us.

Long John lent over the stern and shouted again. "Back off, you young fool! Or do you want me to plug your men one by one? You'll never get close enough to board."

The men must have been feeling a very uncomfortable spot between their shoulder blades and the launch appeared to slow a little. For a moment the officer did nothing, but the sense of Long John's warning made him desist, and he ordered his men to stop. As they rested on their oars he shouted after us, "You won't get away, pirate! We'll have you and your men dancing at the yard-arm yet."

Long John chuckled. "The young master might be right, but not this evening. Sally, let's take something to eat while we've got the chance."

As Sally and Isabel readied a meal, we turned our attention back to sailing. As we steered around the north of the island, we brought our quarter more and more to the wind, a much faster situation. We gathered speed and our wake lengthened.

"We've been lucky, Dick my lad. We shall be right round the island in a little while and the sun will be down soon. It's a good thing for us that the tide's in, or sailing inside the reef would be a deal more difficult."

"But where are we going? The ship will be after us—"

"They won't find us where we'll be hiding," and that was all he would say until after supper. Later, when the sun had set, we searched the shadows under the trees for the creek near which Hawkins had run the Hispaniola ashore. So it was that, resting on the shore with our boat pulled into the blackness of the creek, we watched the frigate sail south past our hiding place. We could hear the slap and creak of her, and the buzz of talk among her hundreds of men.

Long John shook us out early next day with work to do. Sally and I were set to climbing up the lookout hill to search for the frigate. Long John and Isabel would be hauling the boat farther up the creek until it was completely hidden.

Sally made good company. We cut across the island and then took Ben Gunn's path up to the summit from near the cottage. As Caspar and I had suspected when we found the other end of the path, it made a far easier way up. Nevertheless, it was a severe climb and it was fully two hours after sunrise before we sat down under the two fig trees. I searched the horizon with our glass, but there was not a sail to be seen either to the north or south.

The sea remained empty until mid-day when we picked out a sail to the south. Was it the frigate? Whatever ship we saw, we could do nothing for the moment but wait. I stuck two twigs into the ground to take a bearing on the sail. I could not identify the ship but I now knew its course would take it close the west of the island. After an hour, we could make out the frigate. Having missed us to the south, she was returning to try her luck to the north and west. Sally went down to tell the others while I concealed myself on the ground behind the fig trees.

The frigate grew slowly larger in my glass until I could clearly make out figures on her decks. When I could nearly distinguish the faces of the officers, she suddenly put her head into the wind and there was a flurry of activity. She was launching a boat. It was soon in the water and a crew aboard. Shortly afterwards, they stepped a mast and began to sail towards the eastern side of the island. The mother ship continued to head towards the west. I wasted no time in racing back with a warning.

We were saved by two things. Firstly, Long John's good sense in keeping us off the beach. The sand showed no footprints to our passing pursuers. For the second, the sun was already setting, throwing the eastern shore into deep shadow. Our hunters sailed past gaining no hint of what hid in the shadows behind the beach.

I would have sailed next day, but Long John was more cautious. Sally and I watched again that day but the sea remained empty in all directions. We sailed on the morrow, to the south-west.

Homeward Bound

It took a long time to come up to Port Domingo again, but we saw no more of the frigate. We had no cause to hurry and, sitting on a fortune in silver we had another worry, the risk of encountering pirates! We had also to decide what we would do with the treasure. I felt surprised when Long John broached the problem. It was late one evening when we were still two days out of Port Domingo. I had the tiller and Long John sat beside me, smoking his pipe. The boat sailed easily, following the stars.

"You're a rich man now, Dick. What are you thinking to turn your hand to?"

I suppose I did not give much of an answer for he went on. "Can't go back to your old trade, you know, for the crew's all dead or gone. You ain't old enough to have your own ship and I never heard of a rich man sailing before the mast. It wouldn't do, Dick. Where are you going to put your treasure, anyways?"

It may seem incredible to you, but I had not thought where I might put it. What would I do with my hundredweights of silver? What would Long John do with his share? I asked him.

"I'll tell you for why I'm asking," he ignored my question. "I've a couple of things you could help me with. What would you think to living in Bristol?"

Bristol, as you know, is a grand and exciting city. The idea of living there was not one I had thought about, but it sounded interesting.

"You know, I put a deal of business through Bristol at one time or another." He played with his pipe, mostly to watch my reaction. "I need a smart man there just to keep an eye on things for me. Not that I don't trust the shipping people, it's just that they're not family, so to speak. You could set up a house in Bristol. I'll send you a bit of money along with each shipment and you pass by the offices in your smart clothes now and then, and make sure no grasping clerk is taking money out of Long John's pocket. How does that sound?"

"But I don't know anything about offices. Or Customs and Excise. Or anything along that line."

"Don't you worry about that. I ain't about to send you out without a full set of sails. There's nothing they do in those offices that you couldn't pick up in a week or two. Which is more than them scribblers and counters could say about being a sea-man. But you ain't saying no, am I right?"

Indeed I was not. I felt too surprised to say anything.

"Good. For that brings me on to the next thing you could help me with. Isabel. Now I know you're sweet on her." He silenced my denial with a wave of his pipe. "I know you're sweet on her, and I need a gentleman to take care of her. She'll never have much of a life if she takes up with someone out here. She'll always have my name dogging her, and I ain't half stupid enough to be proud of that!

"But if she were to take up with some smart young gentleman with a bit of business of his own in Bristol, why, that would be a different thing altogether. She'd be a proper madam then. She won't come to you poor, you know. I'll see to that. If money was all there was to it, she could marry into any family in England.

"Well, now! There's a net full of pretty fish. What do you say to it?"

My mind was racing for it had never entered my wildest imaginings that I should set up as a regular gentleman and be given the hand of a beautiful heiress. "But will she have me?"

"She will if you ask her right. And her mother and I have talked it over. It's time she left the nest and this is as good a chance as she's likely to get. Wait 'til you're alone and ask her straight out if she'd like to come with you to Bristol. Don't let on we've been talking though, or she'll say no just to be stubborn. You think on what I've been saying."

With that he pocketed his pipe and went below, leaving me with plenty to think about. You may believe that I had no difficulty staying awake for the rest of that watch.

Long John said nothing more when he came on deck to relieve me, or next morning. I noted that Sally and he seemed to be spending the day below decks, leaving us young people to talk. How difficult it was to bring the conversation round to what I had in mind! Isabel would talk about the flying fish, the clouds, the sails, trying to steer, anything but the future. It was not until the afternoon that I managed to reach the question. I told her I was going to Bristol to work for her father and asked if she would come with me. She did not say yes, but she did not say no either. Instead she asked me where I would be living and would I keep a horse. She even wished that I might enjoy my new position. In the end I had to ask her again, this time making sure I did not omit to tell her I loved her and wanted her for my wife. That seemed to do the trick for she kissed me and ran off to tell her mother.

In no time at all, Sally and Long John came on deck, smiling and congratulating us. The ladies went below to cook a special meal and us men sat down for a serious talk.

I am not sure how Long John contrived to land the silver safely. We put him ashore near Port Domingo one evening and then stood off-shore, so we lay out of sight all the next day. When we returned for him that evening, he met me on the strand and ordered us to Bewley's boat yard as fast as we could go. He went off to supervise the arrangements. When we pulled up to the yard we were met by Bewley himself and a couple of Negroes with a wagon. Our cargo was soon unloaded and Long John went off with Bewley into the dark. The rest of us slept on board.

I did not return to the house at that time. Instead, I had to take up the office of clerk in Bewley's chandlery. To my surprise, I liked the work although I felt very green, and I am sure my mistakes were a sorry trial to my tutors. Every Sunday after church (attended with the rest of the Bewley household), I was free to take a pony to visit Isabel and stay for supper.

It was a happy way to live. Plenty to do and good things on the horizon. We were to be married in church by Pastor Bruno who lived on one of the largest plantations. Pastor Bruno was a silver-haired old man who had come to the islands many years before from Switzerland. People said that an unfortunate love affair had driven the young Bruno away but, whatever the reason, he had fetched up in Port Domingo and stayed there. He did what he could to make sure we approached marriage in the correct spirit, but he was wise enough not to fight too hard against the tide.

Never in my life had I been so happy. Isabel filled my waking thoughts almost to the exclusion of my work. We walked together on the grass in front of her house watching the sun set and her beauty seemed to rival it. We were both very young and lived life at the gallop.

Everything I have told you in the past of your mother and our wedding is true. It was a very brilliant affair, not too grand but grand enough for the governor and his wife to attend. All classes of person came and we had a feast in the open air in front of the house. We had presents and best wishes from everyone, and the music and dancing went on long after midnight.

Mr. Bewley eventually released me from his office able to count and figure fairly well. I was at least conversant with the ledgers and files that accountants love to hide behind. Now we had two weeks before we sailed for England, a time that passed like the wind. The last time we saw your grandparents, they were waving to us from a small boat as our ship gathered way and put Port Domingo astern. Their separation put a heavy grief on us, for they were both people I loved, in spite of your grandfather's sinful past. If we had only known what waited for us, we would surely have stayed with them.

We were passengers on the merchant ship Saint George, laden with sugar, tobacco and rum, and bound for Bristol. Tobias Poynter was the captain of her and proud to be so, for she was a tidy ship and well cared for. Captain Poynter was not an outgoing man—few captains are when they are aboard their ships—but he was polite enough to us. He was also to be a great support in our hour of need.

We were not the only passengers. There was a naval clerk called Mercer with his wife; Mrs. Hopkins, a widow with two children; and to our surprise and delight, Pastor Bruno. What had drawn him out of his little cottage by the church? He was getting old, he explained, too old to be riding around his extensive parish. True, Mr. Bonnington (who owned his church) had provided a trap and a groom to get him about, but what the congregation really needed was a younger man. One had come from England, and Pastor Bruno had decided to leave for a while to give the people a chance to get used to him. He wanted to return to Switzerland, and maybe he would stay there if his brother still lived.

The Pastor was in a talkative mood that afternoon. He was full of the mountains of his home, and the foods to be found there, the special scents of the meadows and the friendliness of the people. It all seemed very foreign to us.

He did not dine with the rest of the passengers. Perhaps the motion of the ship had upset him. Isabel and I changed our clothes and went to the galley to eat. She looked very beautiful in her new clothes, and was light of heart and laughing. We pushed open the door. Here started the trail of disaster that was to overtake us. I was immediately aware from the looks that we received that we were not welcome. Mrs. Hopkins stole a glance at us and then looked down, gathering her children to her. Mr. Mercer was looking at nothing, trying to dissociate himself from the impending storm. Mrs. Mercer was the foreman.

I am still unable to forgive that woman, even after all these years. She had a fat pork-pie face with a round red nose. Hard eyes stared at us. "I'm not going to sit here and eat my food with any coloured pirate's brat. Take her away!"

I was thunderstruck. What had we done to deserve such hatred? Before I could frame a reply, Isabel ran from the room. I found her in our cabin weeping bitterly. Although the cook's boy brought our meal after us, she refused to eat or be comforted. I sat by her as she cried herself to sleep.

Later that evening Captain Poynter called me to his cabin. He looked ill at ease, troubled by what he had to say. "I have a problem with you, Mr.

147

Brown. Come and sit down."

We sat side by side on his cot and he lowered his voice to a whisper (there is no more public place than a ship). "The passengers want you put in irons. But this is my ship, d--- the woman, and I'll do things my way." He contemplated the backs of his hands. "You understand that I have to do something. We're going to Bristol, my lad, and if we arrive with all these tales about, you'll be lodging in prison. There's nothing I can do about that. I'll help any way I can, mind. No, don't thank me. It's only right and anyway, Long John Silver would have me strung up if I did any less."

My stomach had fallen to my boots. I had become so accustomed to the thought of our wealth, and of living well in fine houses, that I had ceased to think about how I had come by my money. Captain Poynter was reminding me that pirates are not well loved in England. What were we to do? We could not leave the ship now, and it was clear that Mrs. Mercer would not let us land in Bristol unharmed. It might have been different if we had had anyone in England to speak for us, but as things stood, the very best I could hope for was a long stay in prison while the authorities sought for information against us. And the worst possibility I dared not contemplate.

"Tell me, boy, what have you got on board with you? Do you have any gold? Tell me straight now, for I'm trying to help you. If the Excise open your boxes and find them stuffed full of treasure, you'll be past saving and that's for certain."

"No. We've nothing at all like that. Just Isabel's clothes and our presents."

"Good. That's one thing for you. Now here's the best I can do for you both. Before we get out of the islands, I'm going to maroon you. No, hear me out before you speak. I'll put you ashore on some island or other, give you plenty of supplies and some tools. As soon as I get into Bristol I'll send word to Long John, so all you'll have to do is survive for maybe half a year or so before he comes for you. Once we're on our way, I'll have the crew rouse up your boxes and we'll open them on deck. When that old vulture sees there's nothing untoward in them, I'll seal them up again and leave them in Bristol. You've got an agent there, I suppose. Mrs. Skinflint won't be saying a word about you because I shall be telling everyone that we made a mistake putting you off. Then you can turn up in Bristol later and claim your things.

"There. How does that all sound to you?"

It sounded very well to me. Anything that would get Isabel off the Saint George sounded good, and I thanked him.

"I shall have to say some harsh words to you as you go, but that'll just be for show. You'll have to put me square with your wife. It's for her own good." He shook my hand and I hastened back to our cabin.

Marooned Again

We followed the bo'sun into the sunlight and found the deck crowded with crew and passengers. Everyone had come to see us marooned. Isabel struggled with her skirts as she clambered over the rail and down the ship's side into the waiting boat. Our baggage was passed down after her and then I too mounted the rail. As I dropped out of sight the last person I saw was Mrs. Mercer, arms folded and a satisfied, self-righteous expression on her fleshy face.

Just as we went to push off, the sounds of a commotion on deck reached us. Voices were raised in an argument that was finally cut short by the Captain.

"Let us go!" hissed Isabel, eager to put behind her the ship and the people who had rejected us. "Please, let us go now."

But the bo'sun had stood up and was calling out. Then the hubbub died down and we heard the Captain's voice giving orders. A sailor passed a brown leather bag down to us and then Pastor Bruno appeared, helped by strong arms over the rail and down the side. He was red-faced and panting from exertion.

"Good morning to you both." He beamed at us. "I've come to share your kingdom, if you will permit me."

"You can't sit there, Your Reverence," explained the bo'sun, "That's my place. You sit in the bow there to level us out and I shall row very careful." He handed the old man and his bag over the thwarts into the bow and gently pushed off.

It was only now, with the unpleasantness of the ship behind us, that Isabel and I looked ahead to the island on which we would be deserted. There, behind the bo'sun's straining back, lay The Island. The Treasure Island — again.

I was stunned. Of all the islands we might have been brought to, we were to be stranded back at the site of the bloody crimes I have described to you. Divine Providence had ensured that I would not escape from my deeds, and I would have time in plenty to contemplate my sins. I squeezed Isabel's hand and whispered to her to say nothing.

The bo'sun and I unloaded our luggage onto the beach. The Captain had ensured we would be well provided for. Food, tools, fishing line, even a musket and powder had been added to our things. We would at least survive but we felt very down-hearted as we watched the little boat hauled aboard the Saint George. Soon she spread her sails, and we were rapidly left alone.

Pastor Bruno was sitting on his case, poking at the sand with his stick. "I believe I shall like your little kingdom. What will you call it?"

"Pastor, why did you come? They are right, you know. Long John and I are not good men."

"Oh, I don't know about that. Who is a good man? Of course, I know he's an old sinner. And you too, I've no doubt. But I don't like to see people setting themselves up as judge and jury. Especially when they are going to be cruel to my Isabel. So when they would not listen, I took my bag from my cabin and came to join you."

Isabel flew to him and embraced him, tears flowing down her cheeks. "What are we going to do? What will we live on?"

The old man patted her shoulder. "There, there, my dear. Don't upset yourself. You've got a fine young husband, and he is going to tell us where we shall sleep tonight. After that, why, we will take things as they come, day by day."

He was right, of course. The great necessity in a situation like that is to stop moping and get to work. Things are never quite as bad as they seem, and once you are busy doing something, you start to see the good points too.

We picked up what we could and headed for the cottage. The path, being in the shade of the trees, was still open, but the cottage and its garden had suffered badly for the lack of a regular tenant. The garden ran wild and the fence had been broken by wild pigs coming to root in the vegetable patch. The cottage itself needed a good clean, and probably new thatch as well. It did not look a suitable home for a young bride.

Isabel told me later how low she had felt at the sight of the cottage. The full weight of our loneliness pressed her down but, rather than cry, she dropped her bag outside the door and went looking for palm fronds to make a temporary brush. The Pastor stayed with her and I returned to the beach for more of our possessions.

By the time I had returned with the first load, a fire had been lit on the hearth and Isabel had fetched a tin of water to boil. By my second return she had swept the floor out and a meal of coffee and ship's biscuits waited for me in the shadow of the verandah. We ate in silence for the most part, overwhelmed by our surroundings and with the list of things to be done immediately piling up in our heads.

The very first requirement was to patch the roof. The heavy thunderstorms of those parts come at any time of year and on very short notice. In truth the roof needed to be completely recovered with palm fronds but for the moment I made miniature sheaves by stripping fronds with my knife and tucked the sheaves into the damaged areas. While I worked alone, Isabel took the Pastor to the beach to fish for supper, something she declared she knew how to do.

The fish she caught tasted good, and our stomachs at least felt content that night. As we sat in the fire's glow, the pastor fell to questioning gently until I surrendered the whole history of my doings with the treasure, much as I have set it down for you. He seemed interested in the tale rather than disapproving of it and gave no word of censure.

Next morning we threw ourselves into the tasks our difficult situation demanded of us. Isabel and I being youthful and resilient had slept well, but the Pastor rose stiff and groaning. A more comfortable pallet would be a necessity for him. I must urgently repair the garden fence so the vegetable patch could be set to rights. We needed to secure a regular supply of vegetables for the future, so I set myself to this task first.

Ben Gunn had not been a rich man during his sojourn on the island. It is true that he had been left some supplies but he had little in the way of seeds, so his vegetable garden looked very limited. Neglect and the ravages of the pigs had left little to cultivate but we did find some small tapioca plants and a clump of seedlings that promised to develop into pumpkins or melons. We also had from the ship two different classes of beans.

It was now that the Pastor produced a remarkable gift from his brown bag. He had been taking to his home country a collection of seeds from his favourite plants. He had little envelopes containing the seeds of several flowers that we set aside for the future when we might have leisure for such things. He also had seeds of vegetables rare in Europe. He had Indian corn, tomatoes, peppers and tobacco. These were worth far more than gold to us. We used only a small part of his supply, and that with great care. Our labours in the garden lasted until the fourth day when I had freedom to start improving our house.

On the fifth day we were prevented from working, not by any natural event but by the Pastor. It was the Sabbath and he not only insisted on our resting but also held a short service. We got down on our knees and thanked God for his gifts. I admit my rebellious heart found time to wish that He had not found it necessary to bring us to such a pass. However, in difficult times it is easy to turn to the Almighty and I prayed fervently for help.

So commenced our long period of captivity. After the first rush of repairing and providing, life was not so hard. At least we were warm and dry, and with very little effort the sea provided sustenance. We spent a great deal of our time standing up to our knees in the warm sea fishing for supper. I also spent long periods on the peak of the island, beside a beacon I had built. I was waiting for a passing ship, but I suffered many fruitless days before I saw even a distant passing sail. Eventually, after firing my beacon twice to no effect, this vigil became too disheartening and I became more and more reluctant to make the long climb up to my lonely station. Other duties seemed more urgent and much more interesting.

As time passed on, life began to seem more acceptable to us. It was not so much that things had changed or that our work had made us more comfortable in our little home, but rather that we felt more secure in our island kingdom. Our efforts in the garden had begun to bear fruit surprisingly quickly and we found we increasingly had time to spare. We spent it exploring the island or making small items which were not necessities but which made life more civilised.

We had little to exercise our intellects, so the Pastor took to reading to us from his Bible in the late afternoon before the light went. Every day he would read a little from the Old Testament. After giving us some familiar old tale, he would turn to the New Testament that he was working through chapter by chapter. We all grew to value these quiet interludes.

I do not think your mother studied what was being read in the literal sense. She would continue quietly working at the evening meal, chopping vegetables or stirring the pot, her mind drifting with the flow of glorious words. For my part, I was surprised how much had remained of what I had heard in church as a boy. Now as an adult and with the Pastor's discussions after the light had failed, it was inevitable that I should fall to thinking deeply of what I heard, and compare its gentle message with the violent and ignorant life I had led.

The Pastor seemed singularly well adapted to his strange life. Apart from worship on Sunday and his evening readings, he arranged that two nights a week we would take turns to tell a story. Not a true story, unless we chose to make it so, and we had the freedom to tell fairy stories or folk tales from home, or to embellish some tale we had lived through to make it more interesting. A good teller of tales is a blessing to any community, and with practice our accomplishments increased. I even found myself thinking up stories as I worked so that I might be ready for my next turn.

The Pastor had the strangest tales to tell, taken from his homeland, and this isolated country of snow and mountains became familiar to Isabel and me. It was now that I learnt the true story of his conflict with his brother over a girl that led to his leaving the family farm and travelling across the oceans.

After a lifetime of caring for souls, his interest in ours was a matter of course. He faced a young man steeped in the blackest of sins, and a young lady who had been brought up rather frivolously in a home where the limits of goodness were sometimes flexible. Without consulting our wishes, he embarked on a slow campaign of conversion.

We found him always ready to discuss God and the Scriptures, but he never initiated a discussion, presumably cautious not to frighten us away. However, once a discussion had started, he did not scruple to turn it in the direction he wished and to use it as a lesson for us. He encouraged us to lead his prayers, and I found myself giving the evening reading more and more frequently. That was to save his eyes, so he said.

I do not think he set out to break me, but he did intend that my stiff neck should be bowed and that I should recognise the worthless nature of my preceding life. To that end, he planted thoughts and asked questions that forced me to examine myself. For the first time I started to consider my soul, and to ask if God might indeed receive me at the end of my time.

We had been keeping a calendar so that we might follow the Sundays through the year, and now we began to look forward to the season of Christmas. It is strange to be hearing the Advent stories not huddled in a dark church with the cold wind whirling outside but sitting in the late afternoon sun, lightly dressed and enjoying the freshness of a sea breeze.

If our climate was different, the message remained the same and we resolved to make Christmas Day a special occasion. I spent two days with a musket under my arm, fruitlessly searching for a pig or goat for a table. I gave up the hunt eventually and decided to merely catch the biggest fish I could find. I walked towards the rocks at the end of the beach, where the largest and most cunning fish lived. With a great deal of luck I might succeed in bringing home a fish fit for Christmas dinner.

My path led through the long grass behind the sandy beach and as I walked around a large clump of grass, I surprised a wild sow with her litter. I was terrified because such a beast can be extremely dangerous when she has young to protect. I stood frozen as her black back and tail disappeared into the long grass followed by squealing piglets. I had dropped my rod and picked up a stone to protect myself but she must have been as frightened of me as I was of her, and I heard her crashing through the jungle with her litter following. I hurled my rock into the grass after them and had the good fortune to catch the last piglet just

154

behind the ear. It fell unconscious and unable to cry out for help from its mother. I seized it and ran back the way I had come.

Pastor Bruno was full of admiration for my prowess as a hunter, but Isabel gave me a very strange look and disappeared behind the hut. I went to follow but the Pastor laid his hand on my arm to stay me. "I believe she has something to tell you," he said knowingly, but would give me no more.

That evening Isabel finished her cooking early and came to nestle close to me as we were listening to the Christmas story and its good news. When the Pastor finished, he stopped and looked up at Isabel waiting for her to speak. She appeared surprised at his implied request, lost for words and blushing. "I'm going to have a baby," was all she could manage to say.

I admit to being completely surprised, although there was no reason I should be so. Babies naturally follow marriage but in my youthful fecklessness I had given no thought to it. Now I would be a father and our little family would be increased. "Aren't you happy?" she asked me. Of course I was happy. I was delighted that such a thing should happen, and inwardly convinced it must be the most important baby in the world.

I examine my memories, the places I have been and the people who have shared their lives with me. It is a pastime that becomes more and more indulged in as I get older. For all my searching, I think that Christmas Eve was the happiest time of my life. Pure, unalloyed joy filled me as I sat next to my wife, watching the fire and trying to remember the old Christmas hymns. As we pass through the brief flowering that is human existence, we are occasionally granted a glimpse of another world, perhaps a pale forecast of things to come. Treasure these times and keep them fresh in your mind; they cannot last for long on this earth.

We exchanged Christmas gifts the next day. I had worked long and quietly when I should have been fishing to make a necklace out of jungle seeds and polished discs of coconut shell. It was a primitive ornament but Isabel accepted it with wide eyes as if it had been made of diamonds and gold. It looked very beautiful about her slender brown neck.

She brought out her secrets too. From one of her petticoats she had fashioned a fine blouse for me, so fine I was only to wear it on Sundays and holidays. She had also made a canvas hat for the Pastor.

Our piglet made a very fine feast, garnished with a pumpkin from our vegetable garden. It made a Christmas dinner worthy of the finest house in England, lacking only the wine and brandy to finish it off. So we passed on to the New Year. Our remote situation had long since ceased to weigh on our minds. We were kept busy keeping the house and garden in trim, and there were always new things to try. I had turned my hand to thatching (although nothing like what you see in England) and the roof could now shed the heaviest downpour. I had also constructed a chimney from wattle and clay that kept the cottage much cleaner. While I did this, Isabel resolved to try her hand at pottery, and after much experimentation and a great deal of burnt wood, she made jugs for water and bowls for our table. Pastor Bruno seemed to have little inclination to make things, but loved to work in the garden. Under his tender care both flowers and vegetables flourished, and he also managed to produce some comforting tobacco.

As the new life grew within her, Isabel also bloomed and we all gave much thought to the approaching event. I began to be consumed by a deep-seated worry. After many years of blind compliance, my conscience began to demand restitution. It seemed to me that the Good Lord had blessed me richly, and in truth I feared that the good things might be taken away again. In my distress I turned to the Pastor.

One afternoon as we stood fishing I managed to broach the keg of worry that was burdening me, and the Pastor saw that the opportunity he had awaited had now arrived. Time and his gentle approach had indeed brought me to my knees and he was there to raise me up again.

Many people brought up in the bosom of the Church stray no more than a little in their lives, and so never have to confront the evil that can grow in a human soul. They are born in the Faith and live with it throughout their lives. My case was different, for I had clutched the Devil's hoof and been led by him.

This is not the place to list the profound changes the Pastor brought to my life, but let it suffice that I became a student of his, and resolved to spend a little of every day learning all he could teach me.

Endings and Beginnings

You joined our little family about a year and a half after we first came to the Island. Your mother was very brave and managed to bring you into the world almost single-handed, both the Pastor and I being totally incapable of helping. You were born, just as I have told you, under a tropical sun and you were baptised from water held in half a coconut. The Pastor was your godfather. You were a delight to us all and gave us something to live for.

Life went on. We saw no ships and needed no company, although we often spoke of what we would do when we were eventually rescued. Most of our daydreams revolved around food, different foods like cheese or beef, and hearty wine. The longer we stayed there the more illusory became the flavours and smells of our imagined meals, but we still associated them with home and family.

I was becoming quite lettered under the Pastor's tuition. He had the happy facility of turning study into a pastime and we not only discussed English but also made a start on Latin. (As you know, my Latin is a burden to me but an educated man should have at least an acquaintance with the language.) The Pastor had also contrived to recover my soul, and I resolved to spend the rest of my life working for the benefit of my family and any other person who might have need of me, much as the Pastor had spent his.

Our mode of living settled into a routine of reasonable comfort, and I found I had enough work to keep me occupied but not so much as to burden me. We increased in material wealth as I turned my hand to making our house bigger and more homely. I added two more rooms, one for the Pastor and one for us. Isabel now had a kitchen table to help in the preparation of our meals, which we ate from plates she had made. To make fishing easier, I constructed a small canoe in the native manner, by carving out of a tree trunk. Using this we could fish in the deeper waters of the lagoon, and so catch bigger fish. The Pastor's garden yielded prodigiously, and the gentle climate meant that we did not have the problem of storing food to support us over a long winter. Taken as a whole, life felt very agreeable and we had few cares to worry us.

I will gloss over what happened to us next because the pain is still with me, even across all these years. One day your mother went fishing in our canoe and was taken by the sea. We found the canoe washed up but we never found her. God grant that I will see her again. I shall not write any more of it.

You were only fourteen months old and thrown onto the care of two men, one of whom was heartbroken and the other becoming very old and frail. However, you were far from being a burden to me. Rather you were my reason to carry on when my heart felt like wasting away. In time the pain of our loss became less sharp and our lives regained something of the pattern they had lost.

The Pastor did not seem discontented with his existence, simply his body had become very old and tired. His mind remained alert and his spirit was still strong in his intention of finishing my education as well as he could. I found myself gradually taking over the work in the garden, under his direction. Along with the cooking and fishing I was busy for much of the day, but he did not allow me to miss lessons for six days of the week. He wanted, he said, to make me into a useful help for a friend of his who would know what to do with me and my daughter.

Spirit alone cannot keep old age at bay forever and over a period of several weeks he declined dreadfully. He knew, of course, that his time was coming and he faced it without regret. He taught me right up to his last days, when he set about preparing to depart.

The first thing he did was to change his will, which he carried with him, to leave all he had to you. There, that has surprised you, I am sure. He was not a rich man and your inheritance consisted only of banker's notes. (If you wish to know exactly what they amount to you will have to ask your trustees, but I will tell you about that at another time.) His legacy to me was a letter of introduction and a chance to serve. Writing on the back of an old letter, he commended me to his friend Dr Pulsey, the Bishop of Bath and Wells. He wrote honestly about my accomplishments, generously about my future prospects, and left my past waiting for my own explanation. I treasured the letter.

The morning came when he did not rise from his pallet and I found he had left us. He was a godly man and it is a shame you were too young to remember him. I believe you were not yet two years old.

So, our family of three had grown to four and now we were reduced to two. I do not know if you were affected. You seemed as cheerful as ever while I had to fight my way out of despond. Without your help, I doubt if I would have found the will to survive, so low had I been brought.

However, it is a long road that has no turning and our lonely route finally turned one morning when we went to the beach to catch supper. You were a little over three years old and able to walk and talk, and our passage through the dark trees to the beach was made hand-in-hand at your pace. You saw the ship first, shrieking and pointing your little hand at the black and cream sloop of war moored just off the point. I picked you up and ran frantically towards her, shouting and waving.

What a blessed vessel the Sophie was, and what kind men took us on board. You remember a little about her, of course, but you do not remember what a fuss all those sailors made of you. Nothing was too much trouble for them and you were nursed by those tough old sailors for every waking minute. They spoilt you dreadfully and met your every whim. The bo'sun, a tattooed block of a man with no front teeth and a gold earring, begged a linen shirt from the purser and made you a petticoat, the first garment you had been given since your mother left us. Because of you the Captain (do you remember Captain Holsworthy?) gave us a little cabin and we were often invited to dine with him.

The Sophie was bound for England and had only come to the island to repair some storm damage and pick coconuts. She would touch at Plymouth to deliver the mails before heading up the Channel, and I begged to be set ashore there. It was a glorious feeling to make the Lizard and then to see the Devon coast again.

We had come ashore in the bustle of Plymouth and, after being so long away, I felt a foreigner. We owned very little, no more than the chest that I had brought from the Island. We had some ready silver and, of course, the very valuable papers from Long John that represented my share of the treasure and your mother's dowry. The most important thing I possessed was the Pastor's letter to Dr Pulsey, and so we set off to deliver it.

We made our journey early in September, and as the fruitful fields passed by I resolved to put the sea behind me and grow roots, if God allowed it. Fate had dealt us a blow by taking your mother, but we had been fortunate in meeting the Pastor. He had shown what might be done with our lives and I determined to do my best to follow his teaching. We clattered into Wells and a sudden worry enveloped me. The frailty of human life had been deeply impressed on me in the past two years. What would we do if Dr Pulsey were no longer the Bishop?

I took it as a personal blessing that he was still in his place, though growing old, and waited with some hope after my letter had been passed into him. He sent word to our inn that I should attend him the following afternoon.

I do not believe I have ever been so anxious as on that afternoon when I waited for him. I know you remember Dr Pulsey, but I did not know then what a saint he was and I trembled as I waited. However, he was kind to me. He asked a little after Pastor Bruno and enquired after the manner of his dying. He asked me to evensong with his chaplain so that we might pray for his soul's rest. He then sent me to the bursar with a commission as a clerk. He had made a place for us, all in the course of an afternoon. The way that he accepted us without question seemed remarkable to me, but I later learnt that this was his way. Blessings from God and misfortunes he accepted equally calmly, and made the best use of them.

I was at a loss as to what I should tell him of my past. It took some time before I could lay the burden of the treasure at his feet. By that time we were living within the precinct and life had begun to take on a recognisable rhythm. Although my work with the bursar was completely new to me, my time in Bewley's chandlery helped considerably and I quickly learnt the rote. Long John's papers grew to worry me considerably however, and it was the bursar who sent me back to Dr Pulsey.

My conscience troubled me, for I knew I should have told him everything at our first meeting, and I felt sick as I waited for him. He sat me in his study, closed the door and listened silently through my confession. I had told no one of the treasure or of my previous calling. I had just called myself a chandler's clerk, blessing the little experience I had got of that work. Dr Pulsey heard me without comment and seemed to believe all he was told. He sat for a while deep in thought.

"What are we to do with you, young man? Are you ready to be turned over as a pirate? Hmm, so you say. Even if you are, I doubt if little Rose would want to see her father hung up. And what about the money? To whom does that belong?"

There could be, of course, no answer to that question. The money was stolen and tainted with blood, that much was clear. However, the money that Long John had settled on us was not quite so obviously bad. Some of it had presumably been obtained by legitimate trading, all be it after the initial seed had been stolen. Dr Pulsey applied the practical Christianity for which he was famous.

"Young man," he said, after taking a long time in deliberation, "you cannot keep that money. It would be wrong for you to benefit from it. However, some of the money should rightly attach to your daughter. She had no part in your sins. So what I will arrange is this. Give your papers to me and I will send them to be converted by the bursar. Half of what there is I will place with trustees for your daughter on her majority. The rest we should send somewhere, perhaps to one of the poorer churches out where it came from, to help them turn pagans into Christians. What do you say to that?"

I bowed my head. At least you would be cared for and that was all that concerned me. What was to become of me? "My Lord, may I continue to work here?"

"Of course! You must earn your bread in some calling. Attend to your duties, study hard and if Pastor Bruno's opinion is to be believed, the Church will find a place to use you. Go now."

How grateful I am to Dr Pulsey for taking us in. I am sure we could have survived in some fashion without him, but look where he has led us. It was entirely due to his support that I was allowed to attend the University at Oxford and later, again under his guidance, enter Holy Orders. It was he who helped me to this Parish and gave me real work to do. We must always be grateful to his memory. This reminds me that it is time you were introduced to the trustees of your money. It will not be long now before it will be handed back to you, and I hope you will be pleased with your good fortune.

So, there the story ends. Now you know just who you are and just how you came to be here. The break with this story is almost complete. Until Captain Hawkins appeared, the only other person you had met from those times was Ben Gunn. That is another surprise for you. Do you remember the summer we travelled to Devon to visit Aunt Harding? Ben Gunn was singing in the church choir there, if you remember the skinny old man at the end of the stalls. Thankfully he did not recognise me, although I certainly worried about the prospect.

There is one other person you might just remember. Do you recall when you came with me to Oxford on my last visit there, before we came to live here? We were travelling back and the coach broke a wheel? We walked a little way along the road while we waited for the wheelwright. We walked up the hill and came to that wild cross-roads on top of the Downs, and there sat a gypsy woman, waiting with a small child. That was little Lizzie, though she was a fully grown woman by then. She recognised me, though I cannot imagine how. Do you remember how she read your fortune? Then while you played with her son she chatted to me for a time. She laughed at you and recalled her grandmother's words. "Ah, Dick! And how I wished your second dark lady might be me. Or even your first. Are you happy now your fortune's made?"

THE END

www.ingramcontent.com/pod-product-compliance
Lightning Source LLC
Chambersburg PA
CBHW050753250626
47155CB00005B/2040